My Lady Rogue

A Nelson's Tea Novel

Katherine Bone

License and Copyright Notes

My Lady Rogue
Copyright © 2019 by Katherine Bone
Print Edition
Seas the Day Publishing
Cover Design by For the Muse Designs
Editing by Double Vision Editorial

For more information: katherine@katherinebone.com
www.katherinebone.com

Also Available

The Regent's Revenge Series

The Pirate's Duchess, Novella #1
The Pirate's Debt, Book #2
The Pirate's Duty, Book #3

The Nelson's Tea Series

My Lord Rogue, Book #1
Duke by Day, Rogue by Night, Book #2
The Rogue's Prize, Book #3
My Lady Rogue, Book #4

The Heart of a Hero Series

The Mercenary Pirate, Book #10

Dedication

"I cannot, if I am in the field of glory, be kept out of sight: wherever there is anything to be done, there Providence is sure to direct my steps."

~ Vice-Admiral Lord Viscount Horatio Nelson

This book is dedicated to my rogue and my sons, who show me every day that loyalty and integrity matter.

One

But Chief, midst her heroes, wherever she goes,
She hears her HORATIO's proud name;
FAME's numberless voices in concert arose,
Nor sufficed his great deeds to proclaim—
They sounded, "the Hero her enemies still braves;
"BRITANNIA alone reigns the Queen of the Waves."
~ "Horatio's Death," Anon, *The Morning Chronicle,*
November 22, 1805

Mayfair
November 6, 1805

"THIS SIMPLY WILL not do!" Gillian Stillman Corbet, Baroness Chauncey, tossed and turned under the counterpane, bracing herself as a cold chill seeped into her bones. Fatigue had been swaddling her for days, and frustration haunted her dreams. Something in her was screaming an alarm, and whenever an instinct prickled her senses like that, it was followed by unwelcome news. That was the heart of her worries: who, or what, was about to alter her life as she knew it?

Coals flickered and snapped in the fireplace, giving her bedchamber an ethereal glow. The ormolu mantle clock ticked off the seconds, and every now and again, the townhouse produced a creak, as if settling on its foundation.

Gillian rose to her elbows, grabbed her pillow, and punched it into shape. She laid her head down and fought her swimming thoughts, hoping to find the peace that, thus far, had refused to come.

But what comfort was there to be had when there was still no news of the Royal Navy's blockade in Cadiz? There, Vice-Admiral Lord Horatio Nelson commanded the British fleet as it chased down Napoleon's *Armée des Côtes de l'Océan*—Army of the Ocean Coasts. Nelson was the leader and tactical genius of Nelson's Tea, the clandestine intelligence organization to which Gillian belonged for four years, and no one in their ranks had heard from the vice-admiral in weeks. Was he dead or alive? There was no way to know. Had his fleet snuffed out the enemy or the other way around? It wasn't the vice-admiral's habit to withhold communication with the Admiralty, nor the men who relied on him in Nelson's Tea, for long stretches of time. Fifty-four days was too long a stretch, especially when they had a traitor in their midst, one whose clever manipulations had led to several members' deaths and the capture of another.

Oh, these were the darkest of days, though not the worst she'd experienced in her twenty-seven years. If only she could foresee the ending to this war like one of her plays!

She drew the covers back and swung her legs over the side of the bed. She sat up and lit a candle, glancing once more at the stack of newspapers within easy reach, *Bell's Weekly Messenger*, one of London's distinguished newspapers, among them. Few details had pricked her interest thus far. She'd read the British Fleet maintained 928 ships. Seven hundred and sixteen were in service, of which 131 were of the line—twenty-two carried 30 to 44 guns—129 were frigates, and 424 were sloops. *HMS Victory*, Lord Nelson's vessel, was a ship-of-the-line, a sailing fortress.

She sighed heavily. Where was *HMS Victory* now? *Bell's*

Weekly Messenger had only referenced Lord Nelson once by merely stating that he'd transmitted a letter to the Admiralty regarding Sir Robert Calder, who was facing a court martial.

"A spy, I may be, but I will never get used to this detestable waiting," she grumbled into the silence.

Sadly, there was nothing advantageous about espionage. Spies were forced to lie in wait, and there was little she could do about it. A drawback she should be used to by now.

She'd spent her entire life immersed in one conflict after another, as a child relying on her mother's protection and, after her mother's death, enduring a brutish father who punished her for the slightest infraction. To escape Papa, she'd joined the theater, drawn to its many deceits and pretenses. There, she'd met Lord Simon Danbury, the second son of the third Duke of Throckmorton, and she had fallen instantly and madly in love. But honor had a prior claim on Simon. He had married a family friend's daughter to save his new wife from disgrace.

Gillian had forged ahead, creating a new life with Lucien Corbet, Baron Chauncey, a principled Chouan trained in the protective arts. The expatriated Frenchman had introduced Gillian to a world of intrigue and adventure, and had taught her the skills that heightened her independence. But freedom never came without a price. Sacrifices had to be made. As a consequence, Lucien had died for his beliefs and she had joined Nelson's Tea, a group of over twenty firstborn sons from every walk of life. Her inclusion had not been deliberate but earned in blood after she had been instrumental in preventing an attempt on Lord Nelson's life at Drury Lane.

Four years had passed since Lucien's murder, and Gillian had made a home with her extended family of spies, using her skills as one of King George's secret operatives as an excuse to be close to Simon, who was now a widower. The association benefited everyone, especially Gillian, as she lived in the townhouse let for Nelson's Tea's use. She thrived on danger. But no matter how good she was at keeping secrets, no matter how many balls or teas she attended to gain political intelligence, no one had the news she currently sought. Nelson was even out of contact with the facilitator of his affairs, Alexander Davison, a man who juggled communication between Nelson and the women in his life—his wife, Lady Fanny Nisbet Nelson, and his mistress, Lady Emma Hamilton. Something was very wrong.

Gillian groaned with frustration and put on her dressing gown. In a world seeming to turn upside down, speed and secrecy were vital. How she knew those guidelines well . . . The two components were the keys to success in the world of counterintelligence.

Wrapping her arms about her, she walked to the fireplace, where a low-banked fire burned in the hearth. She curled her toes under the hem of the robe and flexed her fingers across her arms as she gazed into the flames.

"Where is the vice-admiral? Why have we not heard from him?" she wondered aloud not for the first time. News traveled miserably slow under normal circumstances, as dispatches were dependent on wind and weather, but Lord Nelson's messages *always* arrived in a timely fashion.

She bit her lip and began to pace the Turkish carpet. *Botheration!*

Lord Nelson and his fleet were out there, sailing in dangerous waters miles and miles away while members of the *ton* focused on the Duke of Cambridge and Princess Mary alternately singing Italian and English duets. Ladies speculated that pomegranate was all the rage in Paris, instead of pink. Theatergoers flocked to Covent Garden, where John Kemble and Sarah Siddons, two of Gillian's dear friends, portrayed Macbeth and Lady Macbeth. At Whitehall, the Lord Chancellor made remarks about the "Coal Trade, etc." Food was becoming scarcer. Farmers were up in arms. The government had overspent on the war. To the normal layman, life went on while men fought and died for freedom. Was it any wonder she couldn't sleep?

Fiddle-faddle! One thing she knew for certain: Napoleon and his followers were not finished with England. A resurgence of war was inevitable, and if the United Kingdom wanted to survive, first and foremost, they had to defeat the monster at sea. It was their only chance of defeating Napoleon. The Corsican's prowess on land was nigh unbeatable. *The tyrant!* Even William Pitt the Younger had decreed from the Secretary of State's office in Whitehall—the Alien Office—that England needed to quell the French and Spanish ships gathered in Cadiz. Months ago, Pitt had sent for the vice-admiral, requesting a meeting at Downing Street. That had been when he'd entrusted Lord Nelson with the task of putting an end to that Spanish admiral Villeneuve for good.

"I shall give Monsieur Villeneuve a drubbing," Lord Nelson had said before returning to Merton to say goodbye to his mistress. Gillian had also been told that after pacing his garden—what he referred to as his quarterdeck or Admiral's walk—Lord Nelson had prayed at his child Horatia's bedside, then kissed Lady Hamilton once more before leaving for Portsmouth. And on September 14, his ship, *HMS Victory*, had set sail for Spain.

Since that time, Gillian had knelt beside this very bed and prayed diligently for Britain. And yet spiritual things had not brought much contentment. Oh, it wasn't like her to be nervous. She wasn't an inconstant woman, by any means.

She whirled around to face her lonely bed, unable to number the nights she'd tossed and turned in her sleep there. A single candle burned on the nightstand. The flame illuminated the room, casting shadows on the walls, much like the spark Pitt ignited against their foes. Lord Nelson, too, fueled England's fire.

Gillian laid the back of her hand against her brow. *He must succeed!*

She inhaled softly to calm her nerves. *No news is better than bad news.*

A loud clatter erupted belowstairs. Gillian shot a look to her bedchamber door, unease springing to life inside her once more. She glanced at the mantle clock. In the light of the hearth, the hands indicated three o'clock in the morning. Who would bang on a townhouse door at this hour?

Icy fingers penetrated her spine. Moving into action, she closed the edges of her dressing gown and tied the sash about her waist, then rushed over to the bed and retrieved the knife she kept hidden under a pillow. Weapon securely in hand, she picked up the candlestick, opened her bedchamber door, and stepped cautiously out into the hall prepared for the worst. There, her maids, Cora and Daisy, darted toward her, clutching each other. The whites of their eyes glowed in the candlelight.

"What is that terrible ruckus?" Cora asked, wide-eyed. "Who do ye suppose it could be?"

"What is 'appenin', m'lady?" Daisy asked, her voice cracking with fright.

"I do not know." Gillian thrust back her shoulders, a resurgence of energy flowing through her limbs. "But I intend to find out."

"Nay!" Daisy reached out and grabbed her arm. "Let Goodayle 'andle this, m'lady."

"I will be fine." She patted Daisy's hand and raised the dagger in hers for the two women to see. "Go to Cora's room and lock the door until I return and tell you it is safe to come out. And *only* then, mind you."

"Aye, Baroness." They nodded emphatically.

Gillian watched her dear companions scurry down the

hall before turning for the staircase. Once there, she took the stairs one at a time, peering over the balustrade as she descended to the first floor. The pounding came again.

Goodayle had not answered the summons yet, but she anticipated that he would arrive at any moment. Creeping silently down the staircase, she rounded the landing until she stood at the top of the stairs leading to the ground floor.

"Goodayle?" she whisper-shouted into the darkness.

The butler at Number Eleven Bolton Street—her confidant, friend, and fellow member of Nelson's Tea—appeared, ever cool and collected as he shrugged his brawny arms into a black jacket that made his starched white shirt and collar ever more severe against his olive skin. "Is something amiss, m'lady?"

"Of course," she said impatiently. She moved to join him. "Who is at the door?"

"Stay where you are." He raised his hand, a pistol in his grip. "I will handle this."

She gave Goodayle a nod, but she had no intention of allowing him to face the danger alone.

Goodayle wasn't his real name, of course. Many of them operated under aliases. Lord Sidney Wittingham was a broad-shouldered man, tall, meaty, dark, ruggedly good-looking, and fiercely loyal. Such qualities were only enhanced by his rich, noble blood. He had sworn allegiance to Simon and Lord Nelson aboard *HMS Agamemnon*, and then aboard *HMS Captain* when the three men had served together. Simon had injured his leg in Genoa, and after convalescing at home, he resigned his commission to remain with his infirm wife. At about that same time, the Prince of Wales had asked Simon to supervise security at Drury Lane, where he and Lucien had been pivotal in hindering an assassination attempt on King George III.

Goodayle had followed Lord Nelson to *HMS Captain*

before abandoning his honorable title to serve both men by supervising the grounds at Number Eleven Bolton Street, thereby putting his perceptive skills and powers of persuasion to great use. He was good at what he did—exceptionally good. And tonight, she was glad for it.

She rubbed her arms to brush off the feeling of dread blazing to life inside her and seizing her nerves. As Goodayle approached the door and unlocked it, fear of the unknown made her soul quiver. She descended the rest of the steps after him, ignoring the butler's request, and set the candlestick on the foyer table. The candle's flame flickered as the locking mechanism creaked and Goodayle opened the door slightly to peer out. Gillian sucked in a breath and crept up behind the butler, steadying herself for an attack. But against all odds, Goodayle relaxed and lowered his gun.

"It's all right, Baroness," he called over his shoulder. "You may come down now."

"But I am already here," she said from behind him, quirking her brow. Her curiosity, her concern for Goodayle's safety and that of her servants, had motivated her to discover who was on the stoop. "It is cold outside. Do let in our visitors, whoever they are."

Footsteps and canes, noisily out of time, clanked on the marble floor as two cloaked figures, heads cast down, stepped over the threshold and entered the foyer. The pair certainly didn't appear harmless, hiding their identities as they were. She brandished the knife before her. Who had Goodayle admitted?

The two men raised their faces and pushed back their hoods.

Her eyes widened. "Simon!" she cried. "And Seaton!"

Relief and panic clawed at her chest. Why were Simon and Garrick, Viscount Seaton, a man who'd survived captivity in Spain and the several months following convalescing in her care, at her doorstep at three in the morning?

"My apologies for frightening you, Baroness," Simon said, breathing heavily. He shot the viscount a stony glare. "Seaton has news—dispatches handed to him in Cornwall."

The viscount took a step forward and added, "Given to me in the strictest confidence."

"We journeyed here at once to share this news with you." Simon shrugged hastily out of his cloak, revealing he'd dressed in a black coat over a green waistcoat, white linen shirt, black cravat, black trousers, and boots.

Goodayle stepped forward and took Simon's and Seaton's cloaks. "What kind of news requires waking up the entire household and frightening the baroness half to death, my lord?"

"I am not afraid," Gillian said, but her blood ran cold. Had the treacherous murderer hidden among them struck again? "And there is no need to apologize. I am quite eager to discover your news."

Simon glanced at the viscount.

Good God! Something had to be done to thaw their sour looks. "Perhaps you would be more comfortable if we adjourn to the study," she suggested, taking a different approach. "It will give you an opportunity to warm yourselves by the fire. You look quite the worse for wear, Seaton."

"Generous, as always," the viscount said. His unkempt appearance was quite the opposite of Simon's, sparking her curiosity. It suggested hours of quick travel, an activity he'd been warned not to participate in until his equilibrium and health were restored. Seaton, whose alias was Captain Blade, was the eldest son of Filbert Seaton, the Earl of Pendrim, one of their strongest allies on the Cornish Coast. His arrival confused her. Why on Earth had he traveled all the way from Cornwall in his condition? "But I must speak to Goodayle . . . alone first."

Gillian suppressed a shiver and focused on the viscount. "Is the news you bring so terrible, then?" The disheartened look he gave her arrested her soul as Simon took her hand and led her to the study.

"Come," he said with a sad smile.

"Why are you here at this hour?" She gazed into Simon's eyes. "Your guardedness is most irregular."

He didn't answer as he guided her through the study's paneled oak doors, his expression twisting into one of pain. Behind her, the viscount's and Goodayle's voices began to fade.

Simon took the dagger from her and set it on a table before pulling her into his arms and embracing her. "I wish . . ." He caressed the top of her head, then kissed her hair. "There is no easy way to break this news to you, my love."

"What has happened?" She pulled back and gazed into Simon's gray eyes, reaching up to brush his thick chestnut hair away from his forehead. His olive-toned skin stretched taut over his cheekbones and his generous mouth begged to be kissed. "We are alone now, Simon. You can speak plainly." Had one of their members been killed again? She prayed it wasn't so.

Shadows flickered over his eyes, making them unreadable. "Forgive me for waking you in the middle of the night. When I discovered what Seaton had in his possession, I knew I had to see you straightaway. It was not my intention to alarm you or your household. At least . . . not yet."

"Not yet?" Terror sank into her bones. So it was true. A member of Nelson's Tea had died. But who? She grabbed his forearms. They'd both lost loved ones: his wife, her husband. Members of Nelson's Tea had died in the line of duty, too— Lucien, Captain Nathaniel Collins, Chester Walden, and Phillip Cavendish—and they'd nearly lost Seaton in Spain. "I beg you. Do not continue to keep me in suspense. Tell me what has happened."

"Perhaps, my dear," he said, his jaw grinding, "you should sit down."

"Sit down?" Though her heart drummed in her chest, she was not some soft milkmaid scared of her own shadow! "I have stared death in the face, Simon. You know I can take whatever you have to say standing up."

"That is exactly what Danbury told me you would say," Seaton said as he and Goodayle strode into the study.

She glanced from Simon to Seaton, smiling fondly. *"He* understands me."

"Of course I do. You are a very capable woman." Seaton held up a letter between his white-knuckled fingers, then bowed his head with respect. "Unfortunately, I must second Danbury's request. You should sit down. This intelligence will change the world as we know it."

She stared intently at the crumpled missive and its Royal Navy seal. "Is that a letter from Guffald?"

Captain Henry Guffald, another member of Nelson's Tea, also happened to be Seaton's brother-in-law. It made perfect sense that Seaton would be the bearer of that news. Guffald had been charged with couriering messages back and forth to d'Auvergne from London to the Channel Islands. Perhaps—

"No," Simon said grimly, laying her speculation to rest. He guided her to an overstuffed chair. She sat down, then lifted her gaze to his, unease lancing her senses. "We received a message from Admiral Collingwood . . . about Lord Nelson."

So the dispatch wasn't from Guffald at all.

"I see." But she didn't. Why would Vice-Admiral Collingwood contact them, directing covert matters to them, when he had no knowledge of their existence? "What on Earth is going on?"

Two

Her course, overjoy'd at his praises, she steers,

To see her brave Son, o'er the main;

When off Cape Trafalgar, exulting she hears

The Hero's victorious again!

And tells the proud Despot to rule o'er his slaves,

Nor strive with his Queen for the Crown of the
Waves.

~ "Horatio's Death," Anon, *The Morning Chronicle*,
November 22, 1805

GILLIAN SEARCHED SIMON'S and Seaton's faces. They had finally received the news she and Goodayle had been waiting so anxiously to hear! But their expressions provided no relief, and the mystery of the dispatches polluted the air she breathed. Worry gripped her, and all hope that the information they'd received would end her nightmares disappeared. "Tell me what has happened."

Simon and Seaton exchanged a look. "This pertains to Cadiz."

"And what have you discovered?" she entreated, her voice cracking. "Forgive my impatience, but you must read the letter. I want to hear all of it. As it happens, I've been scouring the papers for any hint of the fleet's activity but have learned nothing." She blinked as her mind darted to another thought. Had the war been won? Lost? Anxiety coiled inside her. "No. First, you must tell me how you got the letter."

"Very well." Simon caressed her cheek and then addressed Seaton. "Tell her."

"If it pleases you," Seaton said with deceptive calm. Captivity and torture had robbed him of his formerly quick reactions and his industrious, courageous, and nefarious nature, but for one moment, Gillian was allowed a glimpse of the man he'd once been. "As you know, we acquire wool in Exeter for our . . . *ventures*." She nodded. They all knew the Seatons were the most successful smugglers in England. "I joined my brothers on a trip to our warehouses there, and for the first time since my capture, I took in the night air on High Street." He paused and sucked in an audible breath. "While passing the stables, I happened across Lieutenant Lapenotiere."

His fisted hands made her tremble. Seaton and the commander of *HMS Pickle* did not have a peaceful history. Before joining Nelson's Tea, Seaton had regularly provoked the Royal Navy, escaped detection, and led ships on a merry—and often destructive—chase, only to disappear in fog banks or double around and threaten His Majesty's ships once more. Lapenotiere was one officer who had never forgotten that and had made it his life's work to capture Captain Blade and the *Priory*. But Seaton held another offense against the lieutenant, this one more persuasive: Lapenotiere, like many of his fellows, was a strict disciplinarian with a habit of putting his crew to the lash. He'd been court-martialed for it, proving Seaton's accusations sound.

"That wasn't wise," Goodayle said, moving closer. "Lapenotiere is and always has been a danger to you."

"I expected we'd come to blows," Seaton agreed. "A happenstance I could not risk in my condition. So, in a moment of clarity, I decided to walk away rather than chance a confrontation between us. Imagine my surprise when the lieutenant hailed *me*."

"What did he want?" she asked, rising to her feet.

Seaton lowered his dark-haired head and glanced down at his muddy boots before attempting to straighten his cravat. By all appearances, the wrinkled garment had been tied and untied numerous times about his neck. A sheen of sweat glistened on his forehead, a testament to his inner struggle.

"To give me these." He held up a second dispatch. A wild cauldron erupted in the depth of his blue eyed-stare, and the dark circles beneath accentuated the black eye patch he wore over the empty socket of his left eye. He hadn't slept; that much was obvious.

"After the Battle of Trafalgar, Lapenotiere sailed to Falmouth, evaded quarantine there, and hired a post-chaise," he explained as her heart sunk in her belly. "He traveled all night to reach Exeter. And at the time of our meeting, he was headed pell-mell to London by way of Honiton, focused on the necessity for speed. Knowing how vital this information was to us, I . . . I requested to join him, not wanting you or Danbury to hear this news from anyone else." He scowled, then smacked the letters against his palm. "I suspect this news will be echoing from every corner by dawn. When I left Lapenotiere, he was headed to the offices of the *London Gazette*."

Her mouth went dry at his faltering tone. Lapenotiere had allowed Seaton to join him? She reached up and tugged on her ear, deducing that Seaton had done more than request to ride along. But right now, there were more important questions to get answered. "What news of Lord Nelson?"

Simon's throat bobbed, and his nostrils flared.

She managed a tremulous smile despite her panic, holding her head up by sheer will, and she stared at the parchment, her heart beating erratically.

"There will be a hue and cry all over London soon," Seaton said.

Knots tightened around her heart. Blood thudded in her ears, the pulse bordering on frenzied. She quickly snatched the letter from Seaton's hand. "If you will not simply read the dispatch aloud, I shall discover the source of your torment myself."

"Wait," Simon started, reaching for the missive.

"I have waited long enough. My nerves are quickened to nibs." She gazed down at the letter and she could no more stop herself from peeling open the parchment than catch the moon. The message was from the Vice-Admiral of the Blue, Cuthbert Collingwood Esq., who'd sailed with Nelson into many battles. Collingwood was a reliable man, infamously witty and charming, and his handwriting skills were beyond excellent. His distinctly inked *d*'s were sculpted with decorous tails, and few people, if any, would be able to falsify his writings. No, these dispatches were very real, indeed. "This letter was written on October 22. That was weeks ago."

How odd that her nightmares had started up about that time . . .

She cut a glance to Goodayle. He was just as curious as she was about the contents of the letter, so she began to read aloud. *"My Lord, it grieves me to inform you that Vice-Admiral Lord Viscount Nelson, our Commander in Chief, whose name will be immortal and his memory dear to his country, fell . . . in the hour of victory"*—she looked first to Simon, then Seaton, and then to Goodayle before finishing the lengthy sentence—*"leaving me the duty of informing you and my Lord Commissioners of the Admiralty, that on 21 October, 1805, Vice-Admiral Nelson succumbed to a wound incurred at Trafalgar aboard HMS Victory."*

Her lungs seized, and her hands shook. "It cannot be."

But Simon's and Seaton's countenances remained unyielding, confirming it was the truth. "How?"

Simon put his hand over hers, his touch gently reassuring. "Read on, my love."

Shock numbed her as she studied the parchment. *"My heart,"* she began, continuing to read Vice-Admiral Collingwood's gut-wrenching words, *"is rent with the most poignant grief for the death of a friend, to whom, by many years intimacy, and a perfect knowledge of the virtues of his mind, which inspired ideas superior to the common race of men, I was bound by the strongest ties of affection; a grief to which even the glorious occasion in which he fell, does not bring the consolation which perhaps it ought. His Lordship received a musket ball in his left breast, about the middle of the action, and sent an officer to me immediately with his last farewell; and soon after expired."*

She crumpled the letter in her hands. "Dear God! What he must have suffered—"

"There's more," Simon told her. "And it pertains to us."

Her shoulders sagged as her burdens increased. *"His last request was imparted by his Lordship's own orders, passed on to you through Lieutenant Lapenotiere:* 'Desperate affairs require desperate measures. A tree can flourish after its branches are gone, as long it has roots.'"

His message was clear: Lord Nelson desired them to continue operating Nelson's Tea without him. She covered her mouth with her hand. What he must have suffered, what futile urgings must have flooded his soul as he uttered this . . . How did one handle the knowledge that he would never be able to speak to the woman he loved or see his child again? And yet Nelson had possessed the presence of mind to set aside his own emotions and send a message to keep them focused on their mission.

"As my courier—" she continued reading, her lips and eyes piloted by an inner strength rarely called on *"—Lapenotiere,*

makes haste to London with my detailed communiqués to His Majesty, King George, my Lord Commissioners of the Admiralty, and Lord Danbury, I ask you to assist him in every way possible. The information I've put in his hands is of grave importance to those in your confidence and the Crown. I am, etc. C. Collingwood."

Gillian's composure snapped, her hands shaking. Her heart rapped insistently against her ribs, and her eyes misted until she could barely see. But as she stared at the dispatch, the words were surely there, and boldly written. Lord Nelson, their mentor, jovial and bright, winsome and valiant, seemingly immortal, was dead. She splayed her hand over her throat with disbelief.

"I see it with my own eyes, but I cannot believe it." She tore her gaze away from the letter and raised it to the men who'd gathered around her. "This *cannot* be!"

Victory at Trafalgar, yes, but at the loss of Lord Nelson?

Nausea coiled inside her. Lord Nelson's tactical skill and unfathomable courage were larger than life. He was, or so she'd thought, incapable of dying. Weren't his lasting scars and disabilities proof enough?

Simon pulled her close and embraced her. "I'm afraid everything you read is very real."

"Damned if it isn't," Seaton said. "Lapenotiere corroborated the validity of that dispatch." He paused, looking past her. "The entire fleet spent days in reduced sail to weather a gale that was making it difficult to reach England until the seas calmed."

"Sad business this," Simon said, focusing only on her. He stepped away, taking part of her with him. "But we've prepared ourselves for this inevitability, haven't we?"

Gillian wrapped her arms about her. Death had always been their bedfellows. "Yes, but I did not think we'd be forced to carry on without the admiral so soon."

"Fate is not kind." Simon handed her the second dispatch.

"Here. This is from Admiral Collingwood, as well."

"Perhaps Goodayle should read this one." She stepped toward the butler, who most assuredly mourned Lord Nelson's death more than anyone else present. He'd served with the vice-admiral the longest. To honor Goodayle's sacrifice, she held it out to him.

"No, my lady. You should read it. The admiral is dead." Goodayle's face had paled, and his dry announcement governed the room. "That is all I need to know."

She glanced at Seaton. His good eye darkened with grief, and the same floodtide swept through her.

"Simon!" she exclaimed, overcome with sadness. "Have similar dispatches been sent to Nelson's wife in Bath?" The poor, marginalized woman had supported her husband come what may.

"I cannot say," he answered, "but I would assume so."

"What about his mistress in Merton?" she asked. Dear God, having had Lucien die in her arms, Gillian understood what this horrific news would do to the women Nelson had loved. She stifled a sob. "Poor Lady Hamilton and little Horatia. The child will never know her father." In Gillian's case, that would have been a blessing. There was no comparison between her own father and Lord Nelson, however.

And there were the families of the men under Lord Nelson's command to consider. How long would it be before they read the butcher's bill? The casualty lists were bound to be long. She was dizzy with grief when a sinking feeling she knew all too well washed over her. A vision of Nelson's Tea's first meeting flashed before her eyes: the expectant faces of their comrades-at-arms materializing before her, Nelson's enigmatic and intelligent spectral visage included.

"We must prove, by actively protecting our shores, that our behavior is not dictated by fear, that we have no apprehension of the fate that lies ahead. It is our sovereign duty to gather facts, to keep secret our private signals, and to discover when the enemy will strike. You—" Nelson had pointed to each man and then had leveled his finger at Gillian "—have been chosen. I do not seek another laurel for my post; I seek to achieve victory for my God and king."

The Duke of Blendingham—he'd been the Marquess of Stanton at the time—had waved his quizzing glass, shouting, "Hear! Hear!"

Gillian's heart pounded once more with a furious beat as the answer they'd all given their noble leader, "To death and glory!" resounded in her ears.

"Death and glory," she repeated now, tears filling her eyes as their ethereal response echoed about the townhouse.

Her heart spasmed. Images filled her mind: ships surrounding Cadiz's white sea wall, shots fired, pluming smoke, arching bombs, vaulting boarding hooks, sniper fire, and the shouts of the wounded and dying. She imagined these things so keenly, she could smell the sulfuric odor of burning fuses. War was a brutal course.

Oh, what those poor souls must have suffered, especially Lord Nelson . . .

She swallowed the thick lump in her throat and sank into the chair again, offering Simon a small smile. "The heroic Vice-Admiral of the White has finally found the fame he'd hunted all of his life." Lord Nelson's compassion for the members of Nelson's Tea in his final hours meant they could not afford to wallow in grief, at least not for long. Their very lives depended on it. "We must gather our men to the townhouse."

"You are in shock." Simon dropped to his knee before her and took her hand in his. His brows knit together, and creases formed around his eyes. "You need time to digest this news before we—"

She shook her head. "We do not have time. Delaying our meeting will surely enable our traitor to rally and move against us in our moment of weakness."

"She's right, Danbury," Seaton muttered hastily. "There are men eager to win the Admiralty's approval, men with everything to gain. Captain Sykes is one of them."

"Captain John Sykes?" At his nod, she said, "He put himself in harm's way to save Lord Nelson's life twice."

"He captains *HMS Nautilus*," Goodayle said from his place near the bookcase.

"Aye. He does," Seaton agreed. "The *Nautilus* detained the *Pickle* off the Rock of Lisbon and boarded her. There, Sykes learned about Nelson's death, and being Lapenotiere's superior, as well as one of Nelson's staunch supporters, I suspect he took it upon himself to deliver the news to London."

She gasped. "Are you accusing Sykes of risking his entire crew to beat Lapenotiere to the king?" The whole affair was ludicrous, like something out of an opera.

Simon patted her hands lovingly, earning her earnest affection. "Grief strikes men in different ways."

Their gazes held until he stood. Her stare dropped to his lean, muscular form, her body keenly aware of the vacuum he left behind. He moved to the liquor cabinet stationed in the corner. She braced herself against a sudden chill as he poured several drinks, the sound of liquid transferring from decanter to tumbler filling the room. He turned and offered a glass of brandy to Goodayle and then to Seaton.

"That depends on the man"—Seaton released a sigh as he accepted the drink—"and to whom he owes his loyalty."

"John Sykes has always been loyal to Nelson," Goodayle said before downing his brandy in one gulp. "As are we."

"Aye." Seaton shrugged. "But some men will do anything to better their circumstances."

Including the man responsible for the viscount's incarceration in San Sebastian . . .

Over the past several months, their fellow spies Henry Dundas, Viscount Melville, and Richard Douglas had been scouring documents to discover who among them could be bought for the right price or blackmailed.

"Sykes will not be reprimanded for his actions," Seaton continued. His history with Nelson speaks for itself, and his prior relationship with the admiral will be taken into account."

"I'm inclined to agree," Simon said as he crossed the study to her, carrying two glasses. The proud set of his brows and his height and regal bearing never ceased to make her heart go pitter-patter whenever she looked at him. Now even more so as he generously offered the beverage to her. "Drink this."

She accepted it gladly. "Thank you." She nodded, eager to take the sting out of the shock coiling through her, but she doubted liquor would help ease what ailed her. There were still so many unanswered questions streaming through her mind. "I need to set my head to rights. There are other urgent matters we must discuss."

"What could possibly be more important than Lord Nelson's death?" Goodayle asked. A tense silence enveloped the room. "He is—was—our commander."

"Steady." Simon's jaw tensed as he glanced at the butler. "Now is as good a time as any to bite back your grief, lest you give yourself away."

"Yes, my lord." Goodayle nodded, heeding Simon's warning. "You are right, of course. Forgive me for dropping my guard."

"There's nothing to forgive, old boy. Remember, we all feel the admiral's death keenly. But we must set aside our pain and think clearly."

"Yes," she said. "Our futures are on the line." She stared at Goodayle for several moments. "We have a lot to lose. Given the urgency of our situation, what will Lord Nelson's death do to our men? Will the Admiralty decide to put an end to our covert operations?" She closed her eyes, dreading that possibility. Nelson's Tea provided the perfect opportunity to carry on Lucien's work and be near Simon, and she couldn't bear to think they would be forced to go their separate ways. She sighed and stared down at her drink.

Simon rocked back on his heels. "The third coalition has been unsuccessful. And though we may have won back the sea, I predict war is forthcoming elsewhere. But without Lord Nelson—"

"Do not say it!" Gillian inhaled swiftly, energizing her lungs. The air inside the study grew oppressively thin as they waited for her to continue. "Wasn't it Aristotle who said 'the whole is greater than the sum of its parts'? We set out to defeat Napoleon on land and sea, and we will not alter our course. No matter what has happened, we must forge on as never before. Life offers no guarantees. We know this, and Collingwood's dispatch was clear." Tears filled her eyes. "Didn't he write that Lord Nelson himself urged us to do that very thing while he lay dying?"

The room turned quiet, save for the ticking mantle clock and the flames crackling, hissing, and licking the coals in the fireplace. Light and shadow glimmered over Goodayle's face as he pinched his nose. Seaton absentmindedly caressed the tip of his cane, and Simon stared at the rim of his glass, his posture unyielding.

Were they now resigned to giving up? She wouldn't allow it.

"We have endured assassination attempts, betrayal, and countless forays into danger." She straightened her shoulders and rose in one fluid motion. "We can certainly survive this."

Couldn't they?

Three

SIMON GROUND HIS teeth until his jaw ached abominably. He stared at the amber liquid in his glass, hardly knowing what to say. Hell, he could barely think at all in spite of Gillian's assurances. They'd spent years devoted to king and country, to monitoring foreign policy, galvanizing spies, obtaining intelligence, and outmaneuvering the French, but they were failing miserably at deducing who had infiltrated Nelson's Tea. Nothing in his thirty-seven years had prepared him for the news Seaton had delivered in the middle of the night. He was hardly ready to accept the vice-admiral's death. And yet, he must. He had no choice. Dying was inevitable. No one could claim immunity from this. Still, even as a part of him rejoiced in England's victory at Trafalgar—the annihilation of Napoleon's *Armée des Côtes de l'Océan* was the very thing they'd fought so hard to attain—his heart sank, anguish of the acutest kind piercing his chest. The man he'd looked up to and followed without question was gone in the blink of an eye.

Gillian insisted they move on, but who could fill the void Nelson left behind? He'd been such an important part of the Admiralty and the Royal Navy's morale. Oh, men would certainly rise to the challenge. There were plenty of men in the House of Lords, the House of Commons, and the military who would crow loudly, deeming themselves capable of filling the vice-admiral's shoes. He couldn't bear to imagine the chaos that would soon dominate Westminster because of it.

"Gillian is right," he said. "We must rally. We cannot allow the admiral's death to sway us from rooting out the man who's betrayed us. That must be our top priority."

"I agree." Her support sent waves of contentment through him. His chest expanded as she reached for his hand. He managed a tentative smile, knowing deep in his heart she would do anything for him, as he would for her.

Life had scarred Gillian but not her spirit, and never her heart. She was an affectionate woman, and he knew she was feeling Nelson's death deeply. He wanted to fix this for her, for himself, for his men, for England. His inability to do so cut him to the quick. And furthermore, knowing what assuming Nelson's leadership role would entail, he was filled with gut-wrenching self-loathing. Espionage was a damned hard business that stole from one soul for the sake of another. And he was never without fear that counterintelligence would snatch her away, too.

He raised his brandy to his lips and downed the entire contents, dreading what else they would learn from the second dispatch in Seaton's possession. God only knew what they would face in the coming days.

"We have no choice but to go on as before," Seaton said. "As though nothing has happened."

"I cannot agree more," Simon said. Nevertheless, he wondered if the rest of their group would continue to believe in their organization now that Nelson wasn't there to lead them.

Gillian pressed her lips together. "Do we have any other choice?"

"None." Seaton's sharp retort fractured the moment. "Our work is not finished. Somebody betrayed me in San Sebastian. Delgado admitted it, gloated about it, even. If we do not discover who is against us and why, I fear someone else will surely die."

"Seaton is right," Goodayle agreed. "We cannot tip our hand. You must take command, my lord."

Simon tensed. He shook his head. "But I do not have Nelson's tactical genius."

"Yes. You do." Gillian tightened her grip on his hand and smiled up at him. "You have worked with him personally. You selected each one of us, and your instincts have always been sound." She took several deep breaths as if struggling not to cry. "These are troubling times. Soon, people will come from far and wide to honor the admiral. How unfortunate it is that Lord Nelson achieved such glory but cannot be here to witness it."

"His luck ran out." Goodayle frowned, stating the hard-to-accept fact aloud. He made his way across the room to the hearth, his attention riveted on the sword hanging above the fireplace. No small treasure, the weapon was a reminder that victory came at great cost. Goodayle paused a moment to brush something from the weapon—a speck of dust, perhaps?—that caught his eye. "Lord Nelson knew his time on Earth was limited. That is why he lived and loved to the fullest. Took risks no one else would." He turned to face them, sorrow visible in the lines creasing about his mouth. "You and I both heard him speak of this, my lord."

"Yes." As morbid as it had seemed then, everything Goodayle said was true. "Many times, in fact," Simon answered grimly. "Nelson knew his limitations."

"Because he was an intuitive man." Gillian drank her brandy, then set her glass on the table. She rose to stand, her hand still locked in his, her oval face, delicate features, and arresting and intelligent eyes filled with adoration as she tipped her face up to his. "As are you."

Me?

Uncomfortable with the comparison to such a man, Simon lowered her hand and redirected the conversation to honoring the great leader they'd lost. "Nelson was self-made. He believed many things. If a man worked hard, did his time, followed the rules—to a point—and dared to do what any other would not, he would make a name for himself. I was born into the nobility. *He* earned his rank. And as long as I have breath in my body, I will never speak ill of the admiral or list his shortcomings." He cleared his throat. "He believed in us."

Seaton tapped his cane on the floor. "Aye! Every one of us."

"Always," she said fondly.

Goodayle raised his glass in a salute. "Hear, hear!"

Seaton's voice broke as he said, "I would have died for him." Clearly, he referred to his captivity in San Sebastian and the amount of torture he'd endured without divulging Nelson's Tea's secrets. He moved slowly to the bookcase ladder, his body wavering slightly as he used his cane. "If it wasn't for Guffald and my sister, I would have."

"Once again," Gillian said, "I am reminded how resilient your sister is, and I am thankful for the training she received."

"I fear Nelson's death will be a terrible blow to my sister's husband," Seaton said. "Guffald idolized him. Hell, we all did." He withdrew a book from the shelf and tilted his head to peruse its spine before looking at the ceiling. His throat worked above his rumpled cravat.

"Where are they now?" she asked.

"Who? Oh, my sister and brother-in-law? They've just returned from scouting for the Channel fleet anchored off Brest. A westerly has been pummeling the east with force nine winds, followed by becalming weather and fog. The storm also pounded Plymouth. Guffald sought safe anchorage in Talland Bay, which also gave Adele an excuse to visit our parents."

"I am sure that was a source of great pleasure for all, and the gale explains why it's taken so long to receive news from Cadiz." Gillian sank back down in her chair. Fearing she'd reached the point of exhaustion, Simon placed his hand on her shoulder, to steady her. She patted his hand and gazed up at him appreciatively, making him forget where they were until Seaton spoke again.

"What has been happening in the House?" he asked.

Simon shrugged. He had little to add. "King George, the First Secretary of the Admiralty, the prime minister, and the entire nation have been on edge. The House of Lords debates international trade while bickering erupts from the benches. The world is in upheaval, and none for the better, by all accounts. Soon a list of the dead and wounded will arrive and there will be lamenting in the streets."

"These are anxious times." Gillian tensed beneath his fingers. "Even the loss of one man makes the toll too high."

"Which is why we must ensure that we catch the traitor among us!" Goodayle's face reddened. He bowed his head. "Forgive my eagerness, my lord. I am grateful to you for allowing me to hear Collingwood's dispatch, as bad as the news has been. I am eager, no, *desperate* to protect those under my care, especially the baroness. I cannot do that if I do not know from whom to protect her."

"You are right. That must be our top priority," Simon agreed. "But how do you propose we do that?"

Seaton joined the butler by the hearth and spoke quietly with the man. Simon allowed them this private moment. Goodayle had sacrificed his entire adulthood to restore peace. So had they all. Why, Simon's own niece, Constance, had never known anything but war.

He studied Goodayle. The tall, broad-shouldered, muscular giant was his confidant, assistant, and friend. They'd spent years together on HMS *Agamemnon* and HMS *Captain* under Lord Nelson's command from '72 to '76 in Calvi, Santa Cruz de Tenerife, and Genoa. Since then, they'd served His Majesty and the vice-admiral in whatever capacity the Crown saw fit.

When Nelson had gone on half pay after suffering another bout of malaria and purchased property in Merton with every intention to house Lady Emma Hamilton and their child, Horatia, there, Goodayle had followed without question.

Meanwhile, Simon had resigned his commission to care for his wife, who'd suffered one miscarriage after another, her hopes dying with each child they buried. Her indomitable spirit endured until—

Anger at dredging up the past and a wave of apprehension swept through him simultaneously. Morality and honor had forced him to suppress his own needs and desires. But nothing could change the past, and they could not resurrect Nelson. They still had a chance, however, to solve the mystery surrounding one of their members and why that man had turned against them. Even now, Melville and his assistant, Douglas, were scouring ledgers they kept on members of Nelson's Tea, searching for any abnormalities that might pinpoint who their betrayer could be.

He glanced down at Gillian, desiring to lose himself in her touch and kiss her supple lips. She'd become his shoreline whenever he found himself adrift. She was his guiding light through the shrouding mist of hatred, agony, and despair that plagued him. And he needed her now more than ever.

She stood, joining her hands with his. Her touch dispersed the troubling thoughts cobwebbing through him. He struggled to clear his mind, to bring the restlessness coiling inside him to a halt. Fate was cruel, and duty, honor, and the responsibilities binding them to a cause greater than themselves had separated them for far too long. The fact of the matter was, he should have asked her to marry him years ago, but the time had never seemed right. And now, reminded that any one of them could die in the blink of an eye, he needed to rectify that.

He'd been an unmitigated ass when he'd left Gillian to focus on beating Fouché's secret police instead of nurturing the love he and Gillian shared. One mission had melded into another, and another, and then suddenly, four years had come and gone. The finality of Nelson's death called attention to his own inadequacies. Was it too late for them to find happiness?

Simon loosened his cravat. "Shall we read the other dispatch, Gillian? I daresay we have prolonged our agony long enough."

"Oh!" she exclaimed, dropping her gaze to study it. "I had almost forgotten it existed. Would you read it to us?"

"No," he said. "You are quite capable of doing so."

"Of course." Gillian put her hand over his. "But I would prefer it if you read this dispatch, Simon."

"You're trembling." He brought her hand to his lips. "And your hands are cold."

"I am quite well, I assure you," she said, her voice wavering slightly. "Besides, I am the least of your worries now. Open the letter and share its contents with us."

"As you wish." He raised the missive and broke Admiral Collingwood's seal. He shuddered as if he'd just been the recipient of Collingwood's acclaimed broadsides in three and a half minutes. Anxiety gripped him while he read the first sentence, disheartened once again for what the news conveyed.

"What does it say?" Gillian asked, her touch firm and persuasive, luring him out of the darkness.

"Much the same. I imagine every correspondence Collingwood sent begins thusly." He sped through the details, ignoring the sorrow tightening his chest, and began reading aloud. "Here is something we have not yet heard. *'On Monday the twenty-first, the Commander in Chief made the signal for the fleet to bear up in two columns, to avoid the inconvenience and delay in forming a line of battle in the usual manner. The enemy line consisted of thirty-three ships (eighteen French and fifteen Spanish) commanded by Admiral Villeneuve in the* Bucentaure. *The French and Spanish ships were mixed without any apparent regard to order of national squadron.'"*

"That's what the Frenchies get for murdering all of their officers in the revolution," Seaton spat. "Poor souls."

"Collingwood has provided a complete description of the battle," he continued, forgiving Seaton's outburst. *"The Commander in Chief in the* Victory *led the weather column, and the* Royal Sovereign—*Collingwood's ship*—*the lee. Action began at twelve o'clock, by the leading ships of the columns breaking through the enemy line. The Commander in Chief sailed about the tenth ship from the van, the Second in Command about the twelfth from the rear, breaking through, and engaging the enemy at the muzzles of their guns. The conflict was severe. Enemy ships fought with a gallantry highly honorable to their officers, but the attack pleased the Almighty Disposer of all Events, to grant His Majesty a complete and glorious victory."*

"Brilliant! What more does it say?" Goodayle asked impatiently.

"*About three p.m.,*" Simon continued, "*many of the enemy's ships struck their colors. Such a battle could not be fought without sustaining a great loss of men. I have not only to lament in common with the British Navy and the British Nation in the fall of the Commander in Chief, the loss of a hero, whose name will be immortal, and his memory ever dear to his country. But my heart is rent with the most poignant grief for the death of a friend, to whom, by many years intimacy and a perfect knowledge of the virtues of his mind, which inspired ideas superior to the common race of men, I was bound by the strongest ties of affection. It is a grief to which even the glorious occasion in which he fell does not bring the consolation which perhaps it ought.*" He lowered the letter and gazed into Gillian's eyes. "I cannot go on. This will only distress you."

"You must," Gillian's whispering voice implored as she guided him to sit in the chair she'd previously occupied. "We need to hear it."

He sat down and cut a look at Seaton and Goodayle. Both men stood nearby, equally silent. "Are you sure?" he asked.

"Aye," both men said.

He raised the letter and searched for the place he left off. "*His Lordship received a musket ball in his left breast, about the middle of the action, and sent an officer to me immediately with his last farewell. Soon after, he expired.*" Overcome with emotion, someone cleared his throat. "*I have also to lament the loss of those excellent officers, Captains Duff of the* Mars, *and Cooke of the* Bellerophon. *I have not yet heard of any others. But I fear the numbers that have fallen will be found very great, when the returns come to me, but having blown a gale of wind ever since the action, I have not yet had it in my power to collect any reports from the ships.*"

Simon cleared his throat and flipped the parchment over to read the other side. "*The whole fleet is now in a very perilous situation, many dismasted, all shattered, in thirteen fathom water, off the Shoals of Trafalgar."*

"Good God," Gillian exclaimed.

He squeezed her hand. *"When I made the signal to prepare to anchor, few of the ships had an anchor to let go, their cables being shot; but the same good Providence which aided us through such a day, preserved us in the night, by the wind shifting a few points, and drifting the ships off the land. Having thus detailed the proceedings of the fleet on this occasion, I beg to congratulate their Lordships on a victory, which, I hope, will add a ray to the glory of His Majesty's crown and be attended with public benefit to our country."*

"It is all true, then." Gillian sighed. "The storm prevented us from learning about the battle for a fortnight."

"Yes." Her revelation ricocheted in his brain, but there was little more that he could add. It made no difference when they had learned about the battle at Trafalgar. The result had not changed.

He regarded Gillian with renewed appreciation, studying her high, exotic cheekbones, her slender nose, and the lines creasing her elegant brows. She was beautiful, alive, and he wanted her, desired her as much as he needed his next breath. They'd been trained for surprises like the messages they'd just received. And they'd been schooled in the art of overcoming setbacks. The Royal Navy had done its duty, repelling Napoleon's forces in Cadiz, and together, he and Gillian would single out the mole who'd infiltrated Nelson's Tea before someone—quite possibly even Gillian—was killed. They could not afford to let down their guard merely because the situation had plunged them into mourning.

"Nothing will ever be the same," he theorized.

She dropped to her knees before him, cupped his face, and gazed into his eyes. "Nothing ever stays the same. It is the natural order of things." He watched her bow-shaped mouth as she licked her lips absentmindedly. "Wasn't it Nelson who said, 'We are not guaranteed this moment'?"

He nodded, a tight knot gripping his throat. Gently, he grabbed her hands and lowered them. "He also said, 'Sometimes you must present a blind eye to your enemy.'"

"Even when you don't have to," Seaton said, drawing attention to himself. Skin tugged cruelly around his eye patch.

Or when you have no other alternative.

Simon forced a smile, bearing in mind all that the viscount had suffered, as he watched the skin around his eye patch draw up grotesquely. "My eyes are wide-open," he said. "Nelson's message was clear: 'Desperate affairs require desperate measures.'"

Four

For thee shall spotless Honor grieve,
And cypress midst his laurels weave,
In the hour of victory!
On thee shall grateful Memory dwell
And ages yet unborn shall tell
How NELSON fought, how NELSON fell,
In the hour of victory!
~ "Epicedium on the Death of Lord Nelson," S.
Buller, *The Gentleman's Magazine,* Vol. LXXV,
November 1805

SIMON CRINKLED THE dispatch in his hands, wishing he could cut off the head of the snake—Napoleon—whose ideals spawned men like the one who slithered clandestinely among them.

"What do you propose we do?" Goodayle asked as Gillian pried the dispatch from his fingers.

He glanced down at Gillian, worry nipping at his brain. "Now that Napoleon's fleet has been decimated, the Alien Office will likely desire to divert funds from Nelson's Tea to other counterintelligence networks."

Beaten at sea, Napoleon would redouble his focus on conquering lands and the citizens who inhabited them.

William Wickham, who'd risen from magistrate to ambassador to Parliamentary constituent, had left a thriving network abroad that succeeded in obtaining updates on French troops, their armaments, and operations.

"The Alien Office cannot afford to turn its back on us." Gillian stood, holding the dispatch in her fist. She raised her chin defiantly. "King George will not allow it."

"Pray let it be so." Nelson's Tea had been strictly initiated to protect England's shores. Trafalgar had been fought and won, but the continent was still under siege. The king did not view France with favor. He'd repeatedly called attempts to achieve peace with France, 'an experiment.' As reality set in, Simon worked his jaw. "The Corsican's *Grand Armée* took thirty thousand Austrian prisoners in Ulm and captured their armaments. The situation there is bleak."

"Aye." Seaton almost growled. "The French will not stop until they win or are beaten back. And neither must we. 'A tree can flourish after its branches are gone, as long it has roots.' Lord Nelson's words, not mine."

The viscount moved from the bookcase to the sideboard to pour himself another drink. Goodayle stepped forward, retrieved Simon's empty glass, and joined the viscount.

"The Alien Office," Seaton called over his shoulder, "needs Nelson's Tea." He refilled his tumbler, then strode toward the hearth. "We can do this . . . together. We have to. *I* may be expendable, but the Vasquez family in Spain and d'Auvergne in France are not. They've been loyal to us." He stared at his glass. "We share a history. We cannot abandon them now."

"I refuse to give up." Gillian's beauty, strength, and stamina were at odds with her appearance. Her dark hair draped over her dressing gown, practically reaching her waist. She looked wild, untamable, and perfect. "We must discover who betrayed Seaton and ensure they do not endanger anyone else. We are the roots, Simon. Our reach is broader than any of us knows."

It would be, if they didn't have to worry about one of their own. Someone in their midst had gone to great lengths to poison their tubers, one by one.

"Roots die," he said calmly.

Gillian stared at him as if baffled. She crossed her arms over her chest. "Roots also absorb, anchor, store, and reproduce." She walked a few steps, her dressing gown swishing past his feet. "Trees have many branches. Admiral Nelson's name gave us—gives us—credibility. Perhaps it serves a greater purpose now that he died a hero." She managed a small smile he found hard to resist as she argued animatedly. "You have navigated diplomacy for us, monitored intelligence for us, obtained fake identification and falsified documents for us." She pointed at Simon. "You have kept us safe."

That was all in the past. What was in doubt now was how much longer he could do so. "No," he struggled to say with a shake of his head. He did not deserve the accolades she'd given him. "That was all Lord Nelson's doing."

"Great men do not lead alone." Goodayle returned with his glass and offered it to him. "Lord Nelson was wise enough to surround himself with loyal men."

"Who became loyal because of the admiral's all-too-human demeanor." Simon sobered and reached for the brandy, downing its contents. The singeing heat invigorated him. "My deepest regret is that he was taken from us too soon. Our work is not finished."

"The cost of freedom is a heavy one," Gillian added softly.

"A weight I know all too well," he said. Lucien, Collins, Walden, and John Cavendish, Simon's protégé at Drury Lane, had also paid the ultimate price, dying with honor. He knew who had killed Lucien and Collins; those men had been dealt with. It vexed him that he didn't know who was responsible for Walden's and Cavendish's deaths, though the position of their bodies—when they finally had been located—implied they'd been taken by surprise. Eighteen nautical miles separated France and England at the Channel's narrowest point. Who knew how many French or Spanish spies had infiltrated England? "'A house divided against itself cannot stand.'"

"Yes. This is the time to strengthen our forces," she argued. "Not retreat."

She was right, of course. The enemy had surely counted on them to scatter each time one of them had been buried.

"William Marsden and the Admiralty will deploy more ships to Cadiz to bolster Collingwood's efforts," Seaton said. "If the situation is as dire as he claims, the fleet's surviving ships need added protection. Perhaps we should dispatch Guffald—"

"No!" He shot out of his chair, determination energizing his limbs. Nelson's death played into their enemy's hands. The possibilities were endless, but the main thought invigorating his mind was that their enemy, whoever he was, wanted them to disperse. He smacked his fist into his palm and began to pace. "Joseph Fouché and Bertrand Barère have eyes and ears everywhere. As do we. We have effective agents in the field: Philip d'Auvergne in France, Richard Oakes in the Home Office, Wickham's counterintelligence in Switzerland, Major Colquhoun Grant's Dragoons in the Seventy-Second Foot, and Dr. Edward Bancroft, intimately associated with Benjamin Franklin, here in London."

"We do," Gillian affirmed confidently, her bold stare bathing him with adoration.

Her support pleased him. He grinned. "I have a plan."

Seaton whistled and thumped his cane on the floor. "Now

we're getting somewhere."

"Our first order of business," Simon said, "is to ensure the Prince of Wales will continue to finance Nelson's Tea. Lord Nelson's death puts us in a precarious position. Wickham is no longer in charge of his counterintelligence agency. He is confined to Parliament. If we are not careful, and we cannot get our group under control, that is where I am bound."

"Wickham did not save the king's life. You and the baroness's husband apprehended James Hadfield and prevented King George III's death. Prinny wouldn't dream of disbanding Nelson's Tea." Seaton marched to Simon's side with determined strides. "It wasn't Lord Nelson who got me out of Delgado's hands, Danbury. He was chasing Villeneuve to the West Indies. No. You negotiated my release." He took a deep breath. *"You* sent Guffald!"

"Rubbish!" Simon waved off the man's praise. "I only did what anyone would do . . . for a friend."

Seaton swallowed hard and lifted his chin. *"You* recruited Guffald. You convinced Lord Nelson to give Guffald another chance at serving his country. If you hadn't, Guffald would not have found my sister and guided my men to arrange my cartel. I know just as surely as I am alive, that I am in England, I am safe and whole—" his voice broke strangely, belying that opinion "—because you believed in me, in Guffald, *and* in Nelson's Tea."

Simon nodded gloomily. "However misguided."

"Misguided?" Gillian fisted her hands, bunching them at her sides. "We have worked together for four years. In that time, no one has given us reason to doubt their loyalty until Seaton was captured in Spain." She was right, of course. Gillian's keen wisdom had never failed him, but if he didn't blame himself, who was to blame? He'd ordered Guffald to protect his niece, Lady Constance, the Duchess of Blendingham, the day she'd been kidnapped and Guffald had almost been killed doing so. And then Simon had sent Seaton to Spain to intercept correspondence that would pinpoint the identity of their betrayer and who the traitor worked for. Seaton had nearly died for it.

Their gazes locked, hers entirely too wild and willful, his unwilling to relent. He glanced away in a moment of emotional turmoil and stared at the viscount, his gut twisting. "You suffered unmentionable cruelty because of my lapse in judgment."

Seaton's nostrils flared and fury radiated from his face, but he didn't look away. "Yes," he said, the word fighting its way through his teeth. "You could not have known how dangerous the situation was in San Sebastian. I do not know when I'll forget—or if I ever can—what I have seen . . . experienced, but that has not changed my faith in you."

Icy fingers trailed down Simon's spine. His plan to rescue Seaton had been shared with the entire group either in person or by messenger. Arrangements for Seaton's cartel had not been a small thing. He wished he could have delivered the ransom himself, but Lord Nelson had advised against it.

"I must go back," Seaton said, then laughed mysteriously at the irony.

"What do you mean, 'go back'? To San Sebastian?" Gillian plunked her hands on her hips. "You must be mad!" Eyes wide, she turned to Simon. "You mustn't allow it." It was no use. He had to. The people there were still in jeopardy. "I implore you to stop him. He is a wanted man there. If anyone recognizes him—"

"I shall be more careful this time," Seaton said, tossing his cane and catching it midair, defying their perception of his limitations. "Do not be alarmed. I will not be alone. I intend to take my brothers."

Simon exhaled the breath tightening his lungs as relief flooded him. That wise choice proved Seaton had been ruminating on this very thing for quite some time, and that he was quite sane.

"We sent Collins and Guffald to San Sebastian to meet with Don Vasquez," Simon supplied. "Unfortunately, Captain Frink attacked and put my niece in immediate danger. Blendingham, fortuitously undercover, was forced to step in. Don Vasquez requested we send another agent. Guffald was ordered to go back, but before he could do so, he was injured while protecting my niece again outside Madame Bernard's shop. Coincidence?" He lifted his brow. "I think not. When Seaton sailed to San Sebastian, he was attacked, captured, tortured, and questioned." He allowed moments of silence to linger before he continued. "Someone does not want us to be in San Sebastian. Why? It's possible our informants there are in greater danger than we first realized." He clasped his hands behind his back. "Going back is a wise, gutsy move. But before you do, Seaton, I ask only one thing of you."

"Name it," Seaton said with unnatural ease.

"Wait until we gather Nelson's Tea here." If they intended to cut the snake off at the head, they must act—fast.

"Here?" Gillian exclaimed. "But you said—"

"I'm suggesting we lay a trap." Several of them began to speak at once. He waited for them to finish disputing his idea, then said, "We'll use the admiral's death to draw everyone in. No one will be the wiser, so you need not worry on that score. Meanwhile, Melville and Douglas will continue to dig through our books for any evidence that will point to treason. If anyone can pinpoint why one of us has gone rogue, it will be them."

Melville had once been the treasurer of the Royal Navy, and Douglas was the current paymaster. They were quite aware that blackmail turned one too many agents.

"Pray they find something, and soon," Goodayle added, "so we can end this dilemma before Seaton sets sail."

Gillian reached for Simon's hand. She raised it to her lips and kissed it. "I concur."

"We would be inviting a killer into the townhouse," Goodayle said, stating the obvious.

"We have all killed." Seaton glowered at the man. "That's what we do."

Both men were right.

"We share the same sense of duty," Simon said. "That connection will see us through these dark times. And, need I mention, there are more of us."

"Nelson's Tea will have to be called in," Gillian said, running her hands down her dressing gown.

Simon led Gillian to the viscount. "Go to Melville, Seaton. Explain our plan. He will contact Douglas."

"Aye," Seaton agreed, straightening his jacket lapels. He cocked his brow at an odd angle. "I suppose at a time like this, there's no rest for the weary, eh?"

"The day I have saved every last one of you will be the day I finally seek rest." He took in the viscount's unkempt appearance, dreading what he was asking of the man, knowing the strain might be too much. "Go to Melville. Tell him to contact the others. The news will travel fast from there."

Bells began to toll at the Tower, echoing throughout Town. He cut his gaze to the study window as cannon fire rumbled outdoors, escalating the tension in the room.

"The Tower!" Gillian rushed to the window, but Goodayle got there first, stopping her.

"The bells will alert the city that someone important has died, my lady. People will flock to the streets to hear." His expression grew still, serious. "Someone might see you in your dressing gown."

"Protect your modesty, Baroness. I will go to Melville," Seaton said, his baritone dropping an octave, "and I will return and tell you all that I have seen."

"If that will be possible," Goodayle replied. "I suspect the streets will be impassable within hours."

"Then there isn't a moment to lose." Seaton hailed Goodayle. "My cloak, if you please."

"I was hoping for an opportunity to have it cleaned for you, Seaton. But I see now that will be impossible." Goodayle bowed his head and quickly left the room to fetch the garment.

"Are you leaving, too?" Gillian asked, sweeping toward Simon, her unequaled elegance like that of an angel. Oh, how he needed divine intervention now. "Allow me time to dress, and I will accompany you."

He took her hand in his, feeling the weight of the world on his shoulders as he watched Seaton move to the doorway. He hailed the man, stopping him in his tracks. "Gather the men. Send dispatchers to the location of every known Nelson's Tea member. Melville will know how to reach them."

"I will." Seaton yanked on his gloves, nodding. "I'll send messages to Guffald and his crew. After my brothers share Lord Nelson's fate with my family, I have no doubt he and my sister will be joining us in London directly."

"Notify the Duke of Blendingham, as well," Simon added. "Divide the list and split the task with His Grace. I want everyone to convene here in two days."

"Two days?" Gillian squeezed Simon's forearm. "Given all that has happened, is that even possible?"

"We shall soon find out." He caressed her cheek, then faced the viscount. "I'm depending on you to spread the word."

"Of course." Seaton nodded to Goodayle who then came forward and helped him with his muddy cloak. The two men conversed softly, Seaton shrugging into the soiled garment and the butler holding it away from himself as if it were infectious.

Seaton turned and gave Simon another nod. "I shall return in two days' time as ordered. And I will not be alone."

"Excellent," Simon said. "Godspeed, Seaton."

"To you as well, Danbury. Baroness."

"Take care," Gillian said, leaving Simon's side. "Violence often follows news like this. I wish you to be safe."

But would two days even be sufficient for Melville and Douglas to finish gathering their intelligence on the members of Nelson's Tea? Was forty-eight hours long enough to salvage the lives of over twenty men?

The front door closed, and Goodayle soon approached them. "Will there be anything else, my lord?" he asked. His expression was subdued, but beneath his practiced manners and conviction, Simon knew Nelson's death had affected his old friend deeply.

"No," he said. "Get some rest. The household will be rousing in a few hours."

"Very well." Goodayle bowed rigidly. "I will leave you. Baroness. My lord."

Simon returned the gesture. Doubt, disappointment, anxiety, and defeat clashed inside him just as mercilessly. He knew if he didn't find a way to calm his thoughts, he'd go mad.

"Oh, Simon," Gillian said, sinking into his embrace once they were alone again in the study. "This is a nightmare."

"Yes." He held her close and closed his eyes, relishing the completeness of having her in his arms. Standing as they were, dressed as they were, they could not have been any closer to each other, and yet he felt the distance between them more keenly than ever. Nelson's death and the fate of Nelson's Tea—all they'd worked so hard to achieve—now required their utmost attention. Who was he to long for happiness when the world would soon be in an uproar?

He leaned his head against hers, brokenhearted and re-signed.

"Is this a nightmare?" She shivered. "I pray it is so."

"As do I," he said.

Sorrowful voices would soon pulsate throughout the city. *Nelson is dead! Nelson is dead!* they would lament.

He inhaled deeply, afraid to break the uncomfortable silence. "We cannot fail. Our endeavors have always been risky, but now they rely solely on the Admiralty and His Majesty's good will."

She glanced up at him. "But the Crown and the Admiralty are of one mind and spirit. Surely no one would consent to dissolve Nelson's Tea. Wickham's agents and d'Auvergne cannot defeat Napoleon alone."

"No. They cannot," he said as his stomach churned with anxiety. "When the admiral was alive, though, we were assured support. He was a staunch advocate on our behalf, as you know, so without his tactical leadership and guidance now, I fear our fate is less certain."

"How so?" she asked.

"I am not convinced that our men trust me when I am the one sending them into harm's way. We already know we have a mole in our midst, and without Nelson at the helm—"

"Say no more," she cut in, laying her head against his chest. "You have always given the orders, Simon. I own that Lord Nelson's influence opened several doors to us in the political arena, but you have always been the cornerstone of Nelson's Tea."

He gently pushed her away and lifted her chin, tilting her face up to his. "You and I are not of this world, are we? My gaze is forever trained on the horizon, and your head is in the clouds. And yet . . . we cannot exist without each other."

"It's true." Gillian closed her eyes and leaned her face into his palm. "I am part of any world you reside in, Simon. I am nothing without you, and I will follow you anywhere."

His heart thrummed in his chest like a child waiting for something he could never have as he leaned down and kissed her lips. "What have I ever done to deserve you, Gillian?"

"You went to the theater," she teased, "and made me see what life was worth living for."

"You make light of my words though they are weighted by anvils. What I did to you . . . What you have suffered because of me."

"Never." She pulled his face toward hers. "So much has happened to alter our mindset this morning. It's normal to grieve, to doubt, to feel as if all you've accomplished up to this moment has been for naught. I know. Let *me* help *you*. I will not leave you," she vowed. "You cannot push me away. I will never, ever leave you." Her hands slid up his waistcoat until she cupped his face with her gentle fingers. "Come to me, my love. We will weather this gale together."

The words were hardly past her lips before he bent down to ravish them once more. Her mouth was so hot and invitingly sweet. His tongue explored hers with a savage urgency he couldn't define. She was like a storm always brewing within him. Her assurances, her nearness, and her touch siphoned breath from his lungs like a punishing wind sweeping off the sea. He held her to him, relishing her nearness, desiring to burn away his grief. With Gillian in his arms, he was fearless, and the inner hatred and culpability he'd carried for years found its merciful end.

Desire flooded his bloodstream. He ached for her, hung on her every breath, longing to unlock his heart and soul, bear all in her presence. But the fire he stoked between them would only complicate their lives.

"We mustn't," he said, breaking away from her.

"I need you now more than ever, Simon." Her gaze raked

over him seductively and with silent expectation. "Forgive me for being so bold. If Lucien's and Lord Nelson's deaths have taught me anything of value, it is not to waste the time we are given."

Five

Heir of Immortal Glory now,

Protector of the brave be thou,

In the hour of victory!

Teach thou the valiant, good and great,

Thy high exploits to emulate,

And fearless smile like thee on fate,

In the hour of victory!

~ "Epicedium on the Death of Lord Nelson," S. Buller, *The Gentleman's Magazine,* Vol. LXXV, November 1805

"WHAT ARE YOU suggesting?" Simon asked Gillian, hope hammering in his chest.

"That we give in to the longings of our hearts and console ourselves in each other's arms," she said bluntly. "I want to be with you, Simon. I have always wanted you. No matter what befalls us, my feelings for you will never change."

"And I, you." But the timing of her passionate request . . .

When they finally made love, he wanted everything to be right and proper between them. *Lucifer take it!* He wanted all of Gillian, every delectable inch of her. Now. Here. He wanted her more than he'd ever wanted anything, more than duty, honor, and country. Desire coursed through his body to the bold part of him she had yet to discover, the part of him that would bind her to him forever—or at the very least, plunge her into disgrace.

There hadn't been time to court her openly, not in the way she deserved or that allowed her to be anything other than what she was—a spy. Her reputation as a widow provided her independence, access to certain individuals that a married woman did not have without inviting scandal to her door. But that wasn't what vexed him. Oh, he knew that well. He yearned for her more than any other person in the entire world, wanted to propose marriage, to stand beside her before a clergyman in front of cherished witnesses. But the time had never been right.

Neither of them was a saint. A spy had too many sins to account for and they'd both been married before. No, he could ill afford to lose control now.

Patience.

Frustrated, he ran his hands through his hair. Appeasing his own sexual hunger should not even be at issue. He was a cad to think of his own physical pleasure when England mourned the greatest man who'd ever defended her shores. Besides, they had a mole to catch.

He moved away from the windows, his feelings and desires unchanged. "From the moment I went backstage at Drury Lane and saw you standing there, I fell madly and deeply in love with you." That simple action had taught him how dangerous one choice could be.

Until the day he died, he'd never stop yearning to take what she offered, to lose himself in her arms, to bury himself to the hilt inside her and shut out the world. But she deserved better than that. She deserved to know that the man she gave herself to would be by her side until death parted them, that Society, even Goodayle and the servants, would not cast sidelong glances at her for their behavior out of wedlock.

"Simon," she said, startling him from his musings as she came up behind him and wrapped her hands about his waist. "We have tortured ourselves long enough."

He turned around in her arms, then grasped her hands. They were smaller, more delicate, but just as deadly as his. He glanced up at her face. She stared back with unrepentant longing. He released her hands, then pulled her close, burying her face against his chest.

"I'm sorry," he whispered into her hair. "You have not slept. You are tired and have experienced a great shock."

"Both of us have." She quivered and leaned her head back to look at him.

"Are you cold?" he asked, cupping her face and stroking her chin.

I am a burning flame.

"No," she said. He rubbed his thumb over her perfect lips and tensed with the need to kiss her as her mouth parted. "You cannot possibly understand the thoughts going through my head."

"But I do." Lord Nelson was gone. She was frightened, worried about what would become of them if Nelson's Tea disbanded. She had no way of knowing that he'd wanted to propose, nor that Fate had intervened to foul up his plan. She could not know that he would fight heaven and Earth to stay by her side, that he would give his very life for hers. He caressed her cheek, stalling for time, trying to slow his racing heart. "When I am near you, I come undone."

"Truly?" she purred. At his nod, she added, "Is that such a terrible thing?" Her smile tendered his heart, making it ache abominably more than it ever had before.

Indecision snaked through his body. She was a seductive creature, more polished and poised, using her sensuality and various disguises to full effect. But she'd never used her wiles on him, at least not until today.

Blood rushed to his groin. The pressure building there made it difficult to concentrate on anything other than the woman he loved. Reluctantly, he withdrew from her arms and paced the Turkish carpet, then stopped at the bow window and lifted the heavy damask curtain to peer outside. Saddened by the opportunities they'd lost, he rallied to formulate a plan to counteract the tragedy of Lord Nelson's death.

"Ironic, isn't it?" he asked mindlessly as bells in the distance created a haunting effigy that drifted through Town.

She crept up behind him and rested her cheek on his sleeve. "What, my lord?"

He laughed suddenly, the sound cynical to his ears as he gazed down at her. "A man's greatest victory is often found in death, and it was the *Victory* where Nelson breathed his last."

"Victory," she said, "is what we must focus on. We are alive. Those who survived Trafalgar are returning home to glory in Lord Nelson's greatest triumph. We should be glad of it, heartfelt and happy that one man's legacy will live on long after his mortal body is gone."

Admiration filled him. "You amaze me yet again, Gillian. You shed light on the darkest regions of my heart with but a sound, a word, a look. How do you manage it?"

Her face beamed with tenderness and passion. "With practice," she said, "and patience."

Her complexion was flawless, her skin youthful and smooth, glowing even. She was everything he was not, and more than he ever thought he could be. How had he ever managed to live without her? What was this tangible bond between them, a bond that had outlasted marriages to other people, danger, and sorrow?

His heart thumped wildly as her tantalizing fingers slid up his forearm, kneading, inching ever so slowly higher over the muscle there, her persuasive touch making him come undone.

"I love you, Simon. And love is not dependent on the plans we make."

"I can barely grasp today," he whispered. The world was caving in on him, and everything he'd worked so hard to achieve seemed to be slipping away. "And the day is only four hours old."

"Shh." She brushed a lock of hair away from his brow. "Time, and the worries of this world, are of little consequence right now."

"Aren't they?" He forced a smile and placed a kiss on her palm. "When I brought you here four years ago, I asked for your perseverance, your time, and your talents. So much has happened since then to dash your hopes and dreams. It wouldn't be fair of me to ask more of you. With Nelson gone . . . I cannot say where life will lead me, and you have waited long enough for—"

"Oh, Simon." Her mouth hovered a whisper away, her tempting lips a sweet confection. "Nothing you say will drive me away."

"I do not want you to go, you understand." He drank her in, longing to master her mouth. "I love you, Gillian."

She closed her eyes. "Yes. I know."

Her sigh was an invisible thread snaking around his heart. He had to break the connection before it was too late, before he lost himself. If there truly was a mole inside the organization, that man would not want Nelson's Tea to forge on without the vice-admiral.

A house divided upon itself cannot stand.

What lengths would that man go to get what he wanted?

Simon slipped out of her arms, widening the distance between them. "This life is all I can give you. Once it is gone—"

"We will face that inevitability together," she said without hesitation. "I will never turn my back on you or Nelson's Tea."

Her devotion was clear, and damned if it didn't please him. But someone—and they had no idea who—had begun targeting members of Nelson's Tea for reasons the group had yet to discover. How far did the trail lead, and who would be n

WITH A HEAVY but stubborn heart, Gillian walked toward the sturdy oak doors. If Simon thought she meant to leave him, he was a bigger fool than Fouché or Barère or any French spy believed. She had no intention of abandoning him, of walking out of this room, this townhouse, his life. Not now. Not ever. Simon was all she had left in this world, especially if the group decided to disband Nelson's Tea. He was her life. And she would do everything in her power to keep him from shutting himself off from everyone, including her—or maybe especially her.

Almost an hour had passed since Simon and the viscount had arrived with the terrible news of Lord Nelson's death, and yet it seemed as if years had come and gone since then. How cruel that a few succinct words could completely and irrevocably change one's perception of the world.

In the four years she'd lived in the townhouse, held risqué parties for the upper crust, and dallied among the *ton* to ferret out information, which she gladly passed on to Simon and their cohorts, she'd never once thought of giving up her clandestine existence. She was Baroness Chauncey, a worldly woman often escorted by the foulest of creatures: double agents, spies, assassins, foreign dignitaries, philanderers, smugglers, and gamblers. Inside these townhouse walls, however, she was still the girl Simon had discovered at Drury

Lane, the poor soul eagerly seeking to escape an abusive father and his equally violent and insistent debt collectors.

Now, as her gaze assessed the study entrance, the very same threshold Lord Nelson had stepped through the day he'd come to initiate Nelson's Tea in 1801, she grabbed the handles of the double doors and pulled them closed, determined to see this through.

Her pulse raced. She was tired of waiting, of living two separate lives—him on Curzon Street, her on Bolton Street. She inhaled deeply and straightened her shoulders, then turned back around to face the man she adored with every fiber of her being. He stood at the window, exactly where she'd left him, like a sentinel, the watchman who never slept.

Butterflies fluttered in her stomach. She clenched her fingers and worried her lower lip. Only one thing would ease their pain—love. Throwing her last misgivings aside, she left the doorway and approached him, forgetting everything but the isolated world they'd created in Number Eleven. This was their haven, their sanctuary, a place free from the prying eyes of those who meant to do them harm. At least she prayed it was so. If Simon's suspicions were well-founded and a mole had infiltrated their organization, there was no way to be sure at present. Anyone, or any number of persons associated with them, could be the culprit, her staff included.

Nevertheless, she was determined, and she would always be so. Her love for Simon was an unquenchable fire in need of oxygen. She returned to his side, admiring his lean form. Emotion welled in her breast as she slid her hand over his arm.

He glanced at her, a hint of helpless yearning sharpening his voice. His face had grown pale, emotionless. "What are you doing?"

"I want to prove to you that I am not going anywhere." She moved in front of him, sliding her other hand over his chest, longing to absorb his heat, to feel anything other than the sorrow tugging at her heart. "And neither are you."

"Gillian . . ." His stare burned through her, increasing her need for him.

Carriages clattered down the cobblestones. Voices rose outside. Somewhere in the house, a clock chimed the hour.

Ding. Ding.

He shook his head. "You—"

"Shh." She actually trembled as she placed the tip of her finger over his mouth. "Don't speak, my lord."

His probing eyes widened, and a spark ignited in their gray depths.

In one fluid motion, Gillian placed his arms around her waist. "Hold me," she whispered. "Kiss me."

"There will never be a day when I do not want to," he said. "You are not an easy woman to resist."

"Then don't." Her heart took a perilous leap. She licked her lips. "Make me yours."

He spread his palms over her hips, then pulled her tightly against him, groaning with pleasure. Her body tingled head to foot as tiny rivulets of delight spiraled through her nerve endings at the contact. "You do not know what you're doing, where this will lead."

"I know exactly what I am doing." She felt alive and eager to know that their world had not just come undone. "Kiss me before I go mad."

"Gillian." He leaned his forehead against hers and then, ever so slowly, touched her lips with his. His tongue began a slow exploration of her mouth, and she parted her lips, longing for more of him, urging him to kiss her more passionately. He didn't, exhibiting more control than a man ought to have as he continued to punish her with featherlight kisses. "I should go."

"No," she rasped, clutching him tighter. "Kiss me harder."

"Yes." He growled low in his throat. He carried her away from the window. Soon the wall was at her back and he held her there, hungrily covering her mouth. Shocked by the depths of his passion, by how quickly her body responded to his, Gillian clung to him, drinking in the magnificent, intoxicating taste of him.

He broke away, teasing her by searing a path of kisses down her neck and shoulders. She closed her eyes, glorying in the heady sensation. Her body aflame, she yearned for more of him and bit down on her lip to calm her beating heart.

"Is this truly what you want?" His mouth returned to hers, and he captured her face between his hands. "Speak now for I am close to losing my sanity."

"Yes." She arched against him, nipping at his upper lip. "This is exactly what I need—you need."

"Do not play with my affections." He brushed his lips against her brow. "Not now."

"I cannot. I will not."

"My darling," he said, searching her eyes. "The world is filled with too much heartbreak. What will happen if you lose more—"

"Love is a risk I am willing to take," she said, caressing his face.

Simon moaned.

Gillian made no complaint as he began ravishing her mouth. He grabbed her by the thighs and lifted her in the air. She wrapped her legs around his waist, and he carried her backward. Something must have barred his path because he broke off their kiss and looked away. Before she knew what he intended to do, he backed himself into a chair and pulled her onto his lap.

Her reaction to him, and his to her, had been inevitable from the moment they'd met. The study, however, was not the ideal place for lovemaking. This wasn't how she'd pictured her first sexual encounter with Simon at all. She'd imagined them in her bedchamber, a fire crackling in the hearth, much as it had been those years ago when he'd surprised her during her bath, but Gillian no longer cared. She feared nothing but being denied Simon's love. In his embrace, she succumbed to the intoxicating awareness of him, determined to consummate their love, come what may.

"You possess me body and soul, Gillian."

"Then consume *me*."

Simon pulled her down to his mouth and devoured her lips, making each kiss sing through her veins as he hiked up her dressing gown and cupped her buttocks. The barest touch of his hands branded her skin. She sucked in a breath, tightening her thighs around his waist, kissing him back with a hunger that vibrated through her core.

Balanced above him, she reveled in the strange wild swirl awakening in her stomach. She'd experienced passion with Lucien but never like this. Being in Simon's arms was divine. Bound to him as she was through patriotism, loyalty, and love, she lost herself to the rising fire coiling in her womanhood, a heat so all-consuming she knew neither her name nor where she was, only that she wanted to be infinitely closer to Simon.

She'd never felt so reckless, not even on a dangerous mission. Did Simon feel the same sort of abandon as she did?

She received her answer when he eased her back to open his breeches and stared into her eyes. "Are you sure, Gillian?"

She rubbed her thumb over his lips. "I have never been more sure of anything in my life."

Need registered all over his face, and he freed his manhood. Eager to know him, she reached down to stroke his hardness, trapping his satiny heat between her stomach and her hand. He instantly reacted, drawing in a ragged breath and moaning with pleasure.

"I thought this moment . . . would never come," he whispered.

"Neither did I," she said on a gasp.

"I will ask you only one more time: Are you certain this is what you want? Here? Now?"

His concern for her comfort warmed her heart. She nodded. "Most ardently."

"Well then . . ." Simon pulled her down toward his searing, probing, velvety length. He thrust his hips and entered her.

A rapturous moan escaped her. "Oh, Simon . . ."

She arched her back, her senses afire. He was everything she hoped he'd be and more. The man she loved was as masterful with his body as he was with his mind, and she took all of him, luxuriating in the way he filled her.

"You are just as silky and hot as I'd imagined you'd be," he said, his voice a husky caress.

She fought to catch her breath.

"And you . . . Oh, Simon! Don't stop," she pleaded as the friction generated along his shaft sent an unexpected thrill through her core.

His eyelids flickered open, and he reached for her, drawing her to him. "As long as I live, I shall never be parted from you again."

"Never say never, my love." She laid a finger on his lips.

His mouth twitched, and he licked the tip of her finger, making her crave the taste of him again. Simultaneously struck by the hypnotic power he had over her and determined to comfort him, she gyrated her hips, teasing, tightening her sex, enjoying the effect her movements had on him—and her. His lips parted. He leaned his head back and moaned, the sound of his pleasure toppling her into the abyss. She pulled his mouth toward hers, emptying the space between them, and kissed him, then sucked his lower lip between her teeth.

He kissed her back, making love to her with his tongue.

The woman who yearned to break the mold Society had placed on her clamored to be freed. She arched, taking him deeper as he traced a sensuous path of kisses across the rise of her breasts. Grasping the back of his neck, she held him to her. "Yes, Simon. Oh, yes!"

"You deserve . . . So. Much. More," he said against her, his lips returning to her impatient mouth.

"No." Gillian stilled, and put her fingers over his lips. "*We* deserve each other. For all time." She'd rather die than face a life without Simon. Together, they'd shut out the world and its despair.

He said nothing else as he removed her fingers and kissed her again.

Pure, explosive happiness flooded her body. She gave in to the ecstasy, thinking of nothing else but Simon, his touch, his kiss, his heart beating next to hers. She reveled in the whirlwind storming her senses as he filled her, and she rode him as if their very lives depended on their union. Digging her fingers into his shoulders, she gazed deeply into his intoxicating eyes as a floodtide of emotion surged over her. Tremors of delight and complete abandon took hold. Still, she wanted more. She cried out again, this time in awe. Never had she imagined the pleasure Simon could give her as he drove into her, claiming her, making her forget the years they had been separated. Then all too soon, he stiffened and moaned, and they plummeted back to Earth.

Gillian collapsed onto Simon, sated and not wanting to return to reality. Desperate to prolong their intimacy, she laid her head on his shoulder, feeling the weight of the world bearing down on them. "If I'd known how magnificent this moment would be," she whispered, "I would have become your mistress years ago."

"No," he said, his voice a raspy denial. "I would never

subject you to such a disgrace."

"But we've wasted—"

"Nonsense." He raised her chin until she was looking him directly in the eyes. "We are who we are because of our experiences, of those we have loved and lost."

She lowered her head to the crook of his neck, feeling safe and secure and loved—a rarity. "No regrets?"

"I regret many things," he said, sweeping hair away from her face. He tucked several strands behind her ear, then chuckled softly. "Being an ass, losing my commission, the admiral. But I have never regretted sparing you such a disgrace."

"And if I had demanded your affections?" She leaned back. "What then?"

"I have never wanted a mistress." He leaned forward to trace her lips with the tip of his finger. "I want . . . I desire a wife, a woman strong enough to fight by my side against any enemy."

"Simon." She struggled to rise, suppressing a shiver as she put distance, however slight, between them. Her heart raced. Fate had always been unkind to them, snatching away their happiness. The only certainty they'd ever been offered was the present moment. "Perhaps this is not the time—"

"There has never been a good time to ask you to marry me," he cut in. "But I am asking you to marry me now, Gillian."

"Is that what you're doing?" Her jaw dropped. "But the admiral . . ."

"His death changes everything," Simon said. "But not the way I feel about you, my love. If anything, his loss is a sign that we cannot wait to enjoy the time we have together. We have waited long enough, don't you agree?" When she didn't speak, he added, "I love you, Gillian. I have always loved you. Will you marry me?"

Gillian stared at him in astonishment. She leaned toward him and cupped his face, drawing him close to her breast. "You are sure this is what you want?"

"You have my word, my heart, and my soul. All I have to give."

"And you have mine." She smiled with relief. "I will do anything to help you secure England's future, but I will not risk losing the man I love."

"No matter what happens to us, or to Nelson's Tea, you will never lose me." He looked deeply into her eyes, then brushed his lips against hers.

Six

Destructive showers of bullets fly;
The scuppers flow with streams of blood;
Harsh thunders rend the vaulted sky;
Fierce lightnings blaze along the flood.
Undaunted NELSON foremost stands—
The cause of his Country's and his King's
When, lo! to aid the Gallic bands,
From Hell malignant Envy springs.
~ "Nauticus," *The Gentleman's Magazine*, Vol. LXXV,
November 1805

SEVERAL DAYS HAD passed, and Simon had followed the plans Lord Nelson had made in the eventuality of his death to the letter. Dispatches had been sent far and wide to King George III, William Marsden at the Admiralty, and operatives in the field—d'Auvergne, Wickham's agents, and countless others—though Simon felt sure news of this import had already been dispatched to them. In the meantime, London and all of England mourned. Loved ones waited to hear if fathers, uncles, sons, and brothers had endured the same fate as Nelson at Trafalgar.

Not so for Simon and Gillian, who'd coveted the momentary respite while intercepting communiqués from local spies.

They'd mourned Nelson's passing in a way that made sense to them, by comforting each other, losing themselves in lovemaking, and strategizing on how to move forward without the vice-admiral. And there was still the matter of discovering who had alerted Captain Delgado to Seaton's presence in San Sebastian. He had yet to hear back from Lord Melville and Douglas, and no communiqués had arrived from Vasquez.

Gillian had busied herself overseeing preparations for the meeting Simon had called to discuss the future of Nelson's Tea. If they intended to carry on without the vice-admiral, a vote for him to succeed Nelson would be required. Goodayle had overseen all security issues, instructing the servants on the procedures to follow in light of recent events. Linens had been refreshed, beeswax candles purchased and lit, rugs cleaned, fireplaces stoked to a warm glow, and menus prepared. Nothing had been left to chance.

"Danbury," Seaton said, leaning heavily on his cane. "We are ready for you."

The lines etched into Seaton's face provided ample evidence of the exhausting miles he'd traveled over the past several days. He left Simon's side, moving across the room to sit at the dining table with the Duke of Blendingham and Captain Guffald. Goodayle offered Seaton a brandy, and Seaton accepted the libation. He stretched out his legs, holding his tumbler aloft in salute to the group of trusted companions who took respite by the sideboard: Clemmons, Stanley, Winters, Edwards, Moore, and Randall. Their position gave them full view of the room, and from there, they studied the others with quiet speculation.

Simon's gaze traveled over his men until it settled on Melville, Douglas, and Samuel Whitbread, who was a district attorney associated with the House of Lords. Stacks of financial documents sat in front of them, waiting for their inspection. Across from Whitbread was Dr. James Russell, a Brighton physician who'd saved their lives more times than Simon could count. To Russell's left sat Albert Holt, vicar of St. Dionis Backchurch, a small but wealthy parish in Langbourne Ward. Holt's position, expertise, and friendly manner allowed him to provide intelligence not only from notable parishioners but within theological ranks inside the House of Commons and the House of Lords. His connections to the clergy also meant frequent trips to France and Spain, where the clergyman could access information about Napoleon's and Fouché's movements. On Russell's right sat Jack Chapman, a reporter for the *Times*, who was locked in conversation with Maxwell Hamlet, son of the royal family's silhouette artist, William Hamlet. Hamlet's discriminating eye and attention to detail benefited the team in ways they were only beginning to realize.

Good men all, each serving a critical role in Nelson's Tea. But Simon wasn't sure which of these men would agree to follow *him* now that Nelson was dead. He didn't have the vice-admiral's charm or keen wisdom, nor did he have a plethora of men rushing to follow him into danger.

Holt flashed Simon a pious look that somehow reminded Simon of his father. The similarity niggled at him, filling him with unease as the vicar broke eye contact and resumed his conversation with Stanley Milford and Thomas Forsyth. Simon shrugged off the feeling, attributing it to his own insecurities. These weren't ordinary days, nor was this gathering of Nelson's Tea a typical activation. Without Nelson to guide them, the break in their hierarchy would be viewed by some as an excuse to financially cut Nelson's Tea off at the knees.

His stare wandered to Melville, who gave him a reassuring nod and mouthed the word *ready*.

Simon clasped his hands behind him, then left his position

at the bow window. He walked to the large mahogany table and leaned over to examine the figures Melville and Douglas had calculated. "Are these accurate?" he asked glumly.

Melville nodded. "Exactly as we discussed."

"So it's true," Simon said. According to Melville and Douglas, Milford, Holt, and Stanley, one of Blendingham's men, had run up tremendous debt, something a spy could not afford to do. Repayment would be demanded, and in the wrong hands most likely by way of blackmail. Did one of these men betray Seaton? "Very well, then."

Goodayle opened the dining room doors with impeccable timing. "Baroness Chauncey," he announced.

"Thank you, Goodayle," Gillian said, moving into the room like a summer breeze.

Chairs scraped the floor as, one by one, the seated men stood, and those who had been standing by the sideboard joined the others in offering a respectful bow. She greeted each one, mingling warmheartedly, clasping a hand here and allowing a kiss to linger on her fingers there. "I am obliged to you all for patiently waiting for me to join you."

"And why wouldn't we, Baroness?" Blendingham asked with an effeminate wave of his quizzing glass. "Even bees must wait for a flower to bloom."

Gillian smiled demurely. She wore a silver gown with black lace fanning her neck and trailing down her ribboned bodice to the floor, blending expertly with the damask draperies that cloaked them in secrecy. This was the first time Simon had seen her since he'd left her bedchamber earlier that morning. Her eyes gleamed brilliantly, yet she was calm and collected, her movements giving no hint of the intimacy they'd shared.

The mantle clock chimed.

"Baroness"—Blendingham stepped into her path—"your beauty provides much needed light in the darkness we now inhabit."

She lowered her eyes, peering at Blendingham through her lashes. "A dark world we find ourselves in, indeed." She flicked a glance at Simon. Their gazes locked for what seemed like an eternity before her demeanor visibly changed and her attention settled on Blendingham once more.

Douglas spoke heatedly with Melville while Guffald and Seaton grumbled about Cornwall, and Blendingham bent down to speak to Gillian briefly.

"Gentlemen," Simon began, moving into the speech he'd been rehearsing for days, "it is a pleasure to have you all under one roof. Now that the baroness has arrived, we can—"

"Get on with it," a voice snapped.

All eyes turned to Holt, and the hair rose on Simon's arms.

"Please do not take offense, my lord. What the vicar means to say—" Guffald put a stabilizing hand on Holt's shoulder "—is that we have come from near and far to attend this meeting, and we are quite eager to hear what you have to say."

Simon gave the captain a nod and then glanced at Gillian. Her expression was troubling as she crossed the room.

"Of course I want to hear what Lord Danbury has to say," Holt said stiffly. "We all do. But let us do it quickly. My parishioners need assistance at a time like this."

Taken aback by the vicar's unexpected hostility, Simon faltered. "Thank you for explaining your position so fully, Holt." His optimism for a levelheaded meeting of minds quickly dissolving, Simon frowned at the irritable vicar. These were intolerant times—a situation rivaled only by the death of a monarch—demanding the attention of the Crown, politicians, the Royal Navy, militia, and everyday citizens alike. "I don't want to address the loss of Lord Nelson and what it means to us any more than you do. But we must."

"Sometimes," Holt said, his voice cutting the tension-filled air, "we cannot have what we most desire."

"La! Spoken like a eunuch." Blendingham, immaculately dressed in an outlandish robin's-egg blue coat, gold-embroidered waistcoat, and breeches, waved his quizzing glass in the air, and gave Simon a quick nod. "Allow me to handle this, old man." He approached Holt with his usual swagger.

Simon shrugged. The tête-à-tête between Holt and Blendingham provided an entertaining reprieve, particularly because Blendingham didn't abide the vicar's frequent self-righteous diatribes. The man often behaved as if he was above sin. But taking Melville's and Douglas's report into account, Holt could he be a black fly, a clergyman who profited from harvesting tithes.

Blendingham cocked his hip and bowed with a fanciful flourish, the way he always did when he was up to no good. Except this time, the resourceful duke was working his lethal charm on one of their own.

"Od's fish!" he said, almost hissing as he tapped Holt's breastbone with his spectacle. "Did you forget to go to confessional this morning, dear boy? Or have you been dipping into St. Dionis's sacramental wine again?"

The accusation hit home. Holt stared at the door as if struck. He shook his head, and snickers rumbled through the room.

"No, you say?" Blendingham asked, tapping a menacing beat on his palm. "Strange. Then what, pray tell, absolves you from being insufferable?" He turned to Gillian. "I am forced to admit, I am flummoxed. What say you, dearest Baroness? Have we assembled in your good home in our hour of mourning just to listen to one of Holt's long-winded sermons when our beloved admiral made the ultimate sacrifice? I beg you, correct me if I am wrong. I half expect him to open

Fordyce's."

Gillian paled. "You are not wrong, Your Grace. But this is not the time to fight among ourselves."

Holt lifted his hands and covered his face. "I meant no disrespect—"

"Did you not?" Blendingham swatted Holt's hands away and gave the man his full attention, inching ever closer. "A righteous man like you must have an ulterior motive."

"Of c-course not," Holt stuttered. "I know my place."

Silence permeated the room as Holt's eyes widened and sweat beaded on his brow.

"Anyone else desire to open a vein?" Blendingham asked.

After chasing down the man who'd murdered his father and sister, and kidnapped his future bride, Blendingham had resorted to coldblooded violence. No one in their right mind would cross him now. The members of Nelson's Tea weren't intimidated by Blendingham's peerage or his odd appearance and mannerisms but by what he was capable of. The duke's distracting wig—a nod to his wealth and status—his clothing, and theatrical paint worked all too well, lulling enemies into compliance like a bird of prey and luring them in so he could strike, extracting information or condemning an enemy to death. It was a tactic Simon envied, though he insisted on abiding by the law.

"Ah, there it is," Blendingham said after a long pause. His outlandish, black beauty mark in contrast with his powdered skin, almost dancing when he smiled. "Everyone else appears reverent." The duke turned, then gallantly raised Gillian's hand to his lips. "Forgive me, Baroness. You are the addition this assembly needs—a calm presence in the storm."

Gillian sighed. "I pray that is so."

"Which is as it should be." Blendingham's lip quirked as his brow cocked curiously and he shifted his gaze sideways to Simon. "Now, how is it we are all pitifully exhausted, my dear, and yet you stroll in managing to look afresh, eh?"

Simon cleared his throat. "Gentlemen, as we are now all in attendance and *pleasantries* have been exchanged, may we discuss why I have summoned you here?"

Would Nelson approve of their behavior if he saw them now, in the midst of heartache, clinging to civility? What would the admiral expect Simon to relay to his men?

Press on for England.

Yes. He would press on. For his country, his men, and the woman he loved.

She wore her hair parted down the middle and piled high on her head, a fashion that emphasized her heart-shaped face beneath the glittering candelabra illuminating the room. Silver feathers caressed her dark tresses with light strokes as she moved, his fingers aching to retrace the contact. But it was Blendingham who gave Gillian his arm.

Simon looked away to get his mind back on track. "Though we would all give our lives to see our valiant leader stand before us, regrettably, that cannot be so."

"In one dramatic stroke, we have been deprived of the admiral's genius," Guffald added with a growl. "The navy has lost its beacon."

"I could not agree more," Simon said. Nelson had groomed them all to exhibit the polished mannerisms of perfect gentlemen. He'd offered general frankness, open-hearted candor, and much needed support at the Admiralty and the Home Office.

Whitbread abandoned his place at Melville's and Douglas's sides. "What do you propose we do now, Lord Danbury?"

He gave a slight wave of his hand. "I have gathered you here today to discuss Nelson's Tea. Please—" he pointed "—take your seats." Chairs scuffed the floor until silence settled over the room. "Lord Nelson once confided to his officers that it was his goal to attack the enemy in close, diverse combat. While doing so gallantly at Trafalgar, he opened himself up to sniper fire and was killed. That, of course, you already know." He searched the faces of his men. "I have always sought to follow Lord Nelson's example, but I will not leave myself exposed to the enemy." Simon paced a few steps, hands clasped behind his back. "It was Lord Nelson's stringent desire that we take part in defeating Napoleon, come what may, and I am bound and determined to continue Nelson's strategy without him."

"You cannot be serious!" Holt exclaimed, bolting to his feet. "This is unorthodox. I—"

"Like Lord Nelson, I expect every man will do his duty," Simon said firmly, repeating Nelson's mantra. "If the victory at Trafalgar has taught us one valuable lesson, it is this: unorthodox methods must be used to face down Fouché and Barère. We cannot rest now, even if it is our fondest wish. We must strike while our enemy is vulnerable so that the admiral did not die in vain."

Holt tried to brush past Milford and Forsyth, who pushed out their chairs to bar his path. "Do you expect us to risk our lives without the Admiralty's support? Surely Lord Nelson's death—"

"Have you forgotten?" Simon asked Holt. "'He that would go to sea for pleasure, would go to hell for a pastime.' No. We will forge on the way we have been taught."

"Together," Gillian added. Her gaze locked with his, and Simon knew with certainty that while she referred to the men gathered in the room, she also alluded to their relationship.

"I should have known you would support him," Holt snarled.

"Vicar!" Blendingham tapped his spectacle on his glass, gaining everyone's attention. "You need a lesson in humility."

Gillian's jaw twitched. She moved away from the duke, a

mixture of worry and something Simon couldn't pinpoint registering on her face.

Simon glanced around the room, the heightened tension stealing his breath. "Nelson once said, 'The enemy will not have long reason to boast,' that he would 'completely annihilate the whole of them.'"

"In this," Gillian said, taking a few measured steps, "he was successful. Lord Nelson will be long celebrated as the first hero of our age, and it is only fitting that we honor him. We cannot give up now. Not when Fouché's spies still roam about London."

"Hear! Hear!" Shouts filtered through the room.

Simon smiled. Gillian was proficient at steering the conversation toward the topic he needed and wanted to address. "Nelson's reputation, his very presence, forced greater opposition from the enemy. And yet, as we can attest, men flocked to greet him, forgetting rank and file. In faith, when his body returns to London, you shall see a crush unlike any you've ever witnessed before."

"But . . ." Holt's intake of breath was swift. "Do you mean to say that he wasn't buried at sea?"

"Good heavens, no!" Gillian clutched a hand to her breast, her surprise and disgust clearly evident. "Why would you suggest such a thing?"

"It is a normal occurrence for the navy." Holt fidgeted. "I assumed . . ."

"The logistics of transporting a body," Russell said, examining their faces, "for that length of time requires—"

"Unusual diligence," Simon finished for him. "A delicate matter his men have surely taken care of out of respect for their leader."

"We are not here to debate the state of the admiral's remains," Gillian said, glancing at the ceiling, "but to honor him by forging onward in his stead."

Holt was not appeased. His agitation only grew. "Trafalgar has ended Napoleon's conquest of the British Isles. Our shores are safe. Nothing more is required from us. I suggest we disband and allow Wickham's and Sir Arthur Wellesley's men to handle things from here."

"Wickham does not deal with espionage anymore," Melville argued. "And Sir Arthur is in the field."

Angry outbursts filled the room as men debated Holt's ill-timed proposal.

"If we abandon our country, who will be left to guard England's shores?" Gillian's eyes glinted strangely amid the chaos. Her shoulders were squared, her fingers twitching over creases in her gown as she walked toward Simon. "We cannot abandon our fellows now."

"Hear! Hear!" Blendingham shouted. "This is the time to band together, not turn our backs on our own countrymen."

Holt began pacing. He shook his fist, garnering Blendingham's annoyance. "Are you suggesting I have changed my colors, Your Grace?"

"Do not put words into my mouth, Vicar," Blendingham retorted.

Tension filled the room, forcing Simon to wonder why Holt was at the root of it. Holt was a sly, intelligent man operating under the sponsorship of Lord Guildford in the House of Lords, a more power-hungry politician one would be hard-pressed to find. The vicarage at St. Dionis Backchurch fell under Guildford's jurisdiction, as the area catered to rich parishioners who donated monetary resources to the poor. The connection allowed Holt to come and go without question, placing the vicar strategically within Guildford's inner circle. It was an association not easily won, a fact none of them would likely forget given the hierarchy of clergymen and the Church as a whole. It was especially so since the Admiralty's dwindling funds had recently come under investigation. There was leverage to be had in religious circles, an advantage that provided Nelson's Tea with inside knowledge of what went on in the dioceses throughout London, as well as in the House of Lords. And yet the church had a long history of corruption and vice.

"Lord Nelson's victory at Trafalgar is just the beginning," Simon said, looking Holt square in the eyes. "His last signal will be a rally cry for our foot soldiers. Surely you understand England, the Admiralty, the prime minister, and the king face other threats just as deadly and ruinous than an assault on our shores. French spies continue to extort information and funds from our banks. Napoleon's fleet in Boulogne may be depleted, but the Coriscan's army is still advancing on the continent."

"Without Lord Nelson, how will the Admiralty Board protect us?" Holt demanded. "Have they offered guarantees?"

Several men murmured in response to the questions he posed.

"The Alien Office has a commendable history, and Lords Melville and Danbury still have connections, Vicar," Gillian said. "There is no need to jump to conclusions."

"Whatever they decide, it will not be enough," Holt replied.

"How so?" Simon asked. Why was the man being so combative? The back of his neck prickled with unease. "Lord Nelson's death has been quite a shock. Believe me when I say, I hear your concerns—"

"Do you? Hear my concerns?" Holt pointed nervously to the financials that Melville and Douglas had retrieved from the Admiralty. "What is in those ledgers?"

"We have been investigating our members," Melville quickly supplied.

Milford's eyes widened, exhibiting alarm. And with good reason. He'd lost a great deal of blunt on the races at

Tattersalls.

"Standard procedure," Stanley said from his position near the sideboard. He'd lost his wages at silver hells, small-time gambling clubs for the lower classes. Stanley quirked his brow and then shrugged. "No alarm be needed."

"I am not *alarmed*," the vicar said, lowering his voice. That wasn't the impression he gave them. "But if my participation in Nelson's Tea ever reaches Lord Guildford's ears, I will lose my position in the Church. I have done things . . . Things no clergyman should ever contemplate. No." He shook his head. "Napoleon's fleet has been defeated; England is safe. We have won our objective. Now is the time to disperse and get on with the very act of living our lives."

"Tell that to the men who are counting on our counterintelligence." Gillian picked up a ledger and thumbed through it before tossing it back on the table. "I am surprised at you, Vicar. I never expected you, of all people, to turn your back on helpless men, women, and children, like those enduring unspeakable depravity in Spain. You have seen firsthand what the citizens of San Sebastian are experiencing, and yet you would turn your back on them?"

"Sadly, I must. I have spent my entire life caring for those in need." Holt had no reason to fear the files in Melville's possession would make it into the wrong hands. Lord Guildford might be the head of Holt's diocese, but he is an Englishman first and foremost. Besides, procedures had been put in place to thwart such a coup d'état. Unless Holt knew something they did not. Unless . . .

"You are welcome to leave the group, *if* that is your wish," Simon told him. "You have my word: your information will remain confidential and your name will never be mentioned again."

Holt rubbed his hands together, then swiped them through his thick, jet-black hair. "That is not what I am worried about, my lord."

"Then what?" Gillian asked. "We are all in this together."

"Not exactly." Seaton had spoken, and his good eye glinted wildly as he narrowed it on the vicar. "Who among us sailed to Spain and returned unscathed within the past year?" He pointed his finger at Holt then scraped his boots on the floor—an Oxford way of expressing one's dislike of a preacher. "Holt is the only one, besides me and Guffald, who has intimately dealt with Spain."

"Yes. I have been to Spain," the vicar supplied. "I have been in constant contact with the priests at San Vicente and the Basilica of Santa María in San Sebastian. I also worked diligently to secure your release, my lord." Holt's throat bobbed perceptibly. He gave Seaton what seemed to be a forced smile, then repositioned himself, an action that brought him closer to Gillian. "I deserve a sainthood for it."

Gillian flinched. Did she know something Simon didn't? Before he could ask her, the spiritual flesh-broker began singing his own praises.

"I have helped rescue the doomed souls that Don Vasquez and his family have liberated," he continued. "A small price to pay for passing information to you about the French envoy Admiral Roche and his dealings with the Spanish navy."

"Commendable, of course," Guffald said, voicing his approval. "I daresay you were quite helpful in procuring Seaton's release. We couldn't have done it without you, Vicar."

As much as Simon enjoyed congratulating his men, this conversation was getting them nowhere. "Gentlemen," he said, nodding to Gillian. "My lady." He returned his attention to Holt and bowed his head. "Let us put this matter to a vote. Shall we continue?"

"Hear! Hear!" most of them cheered.

Holt pressed his lips into a thin line. "But the admiral is gone."

"We do not need to be reminded," Seaton snapped.

"No. We do not." Simon meant to close out this conversation the best way he knew how. "Gentlemen, let us ruminate on everything that has been said. We have all night to discuss practical matters. But first, I'd like to celebrate the man responsible for our alliance." He turned to Gillian and gave her a slight bow. "Baroness, will you do the honors?"

"As you wish," she said, her sultry voice hiding the wariness reflected in her eyes. At her nod, three servants came forward to pour port into the crystal glasses stationed around the dining table. The vice-admiral enjoyed his port. When the last goblet had been filled, Gillian raised her glass and tipped her head. "To an unconquerable spirit—" She stopped, her voice quivering. "To the immortal memory of Lord Nelson, and to . . . victory."

"Hear, hear." The lackluster response was followed by intense silence.

Simon sought to lessen the void. "Our devastating loss weighs heavily on our mission and our country, and on us. In a few moments, let us revisit one of Nelson's favorite pastimes: we will sup together."

Milford choked on his port. "M-My lord, you cannot expect us to eat at a time like this."

"Certainly not!" Holt pursed his lips. "The entire country is in an uproar, and we have our normal duties to attend."

Stanley said, "That 'as never stopped ye from eatin' at m'lady's table before." His suggestion drew several loud guffaws from Seaton's men.

"How dare you speak, you filthy pirate," Holt shouted.

Stanley raised the back of his hand and held up two fingers, giving Holt a profane gesture. Several men standing beside him snickered.

"You do this to me?" The vicar's eyes widened, and he gasped. "I am a man of God!"

A shrill whistle from Guffald brought an end to their insults. When everyone in the room quieted, he nodded to Simon. "Proceed, my lord."

"Hear, hear, Captain!" Blendingham exclaimed, choosing that particular moment to speak up. "More port, Holt?" The duke raised his spectacle and flashed a wicked smile. "It does a capital job of abolishing fear."

"I am not afraid, Your Grace." Holt straightened. "I'm bloody angry!"

"And I want to know why." Blendingham's brows rose to his white powdered wig, his beauty mark bobbed, and fake, throaty, good-humored laughter erupted from his throat. He waved his quizzing glass in the air. "Gentlemen, why are we quarreling? We are all men of character, judges of fallacy, schemers of persuasion. That is what put us in the admiral's good graces from the very beginning." He smiled. "There is no reason for us to try to outwit one another."

"Outwit—"

"Well said, Your Grace." Gillian interrupted Holt as if she was attempting to calm the man down. She raised her glass to the duke in a conspiratorial salute. "Thank you."

"The pleasure's all mine," Blendingham said, winking. "Bickering makes a dead bore."

Holt's color heightened again. "Are you threatening me, Your Grace?"

"If I were . . ." Blendingham tipped his head, allowing Holt to fill in the blanks.

"Gentlemen." Simon raised his hands. "Blendingham is right on one account." His intuition hinted that Holt was either sick or crazed. Simon didn't know which. What was the vicar thinking to take on Blendingham? "Fighting amongst ourselves will not help any of us. In fact, I suspect that such behavior is the enemy's only hope now that Nelson has been cut down in his prime."

Melville, who'd been jotting down several notations in his ledger, absentmindedly twirled his feathered quill between his thumb and forefinger. "How will we ever move forward if we cannot get along?"

"Which is my point exactly," Holt said. "Lord Nelson banded us together."

"Danbury had a say in that if I recall." In a moment of clumsiness—or was it nerves?—Milford knocked over his brandy, then scrambled to wipe up the liquid seeping toward Melville's books.

Melville grumbled as he and Douglas started snatching papers and ledgers into their arms.

Holt ignored the chaos. "We have sacrificed enough for England, don't you agree, Milford?" He straightened his lapels and puffed up his chest. "Each of us has an occupation outside this room that has been neglected for too long."

"Take care, sir!" Guffald pushed out of his chair. "We all agreed to become spies."

Holt glared at the captain. "Shouldn't *you* have been with the admiral at Trafalgar?"

"You go too far," Guffald warned. "I have done my part. And Lord Seaton and I bear the scars to prove it."

"We all do," the duke offered, rising to his feet. "And we will continue to serve Danbury without the good admiral, God rest his soul."

Holt made the sign of the cross, but his slow smile never quite reached his feral-looking eyes. "That is easy for you to say, Your Grace," the vicar continued erroneously. "You are plump in the pocket with little else to keep you occupied. While we—"

"What are you implying?" Blendingham squared his shoulders.

Chapman, an erstwhile newspaperman, darted to his feet. "You, of all people, know the duke sacrifices his dignity for our cause every single day."

"Thank you, Chapman." Simon raised his hand, motioning for Chapman to stand down. His Grace was a man of many faces—nobleman, pirate, dandy, spy. People seldom knew which personality they were going to get at any given time. But not because the man was tetched or wicked or a fool. Far from it. And they all knew it, which made Holt's attack on the duke's character all the more perplexing.

Muscles twitched in Blendingham's jaw as he took several steps toward Holt. Simon tensed. The room quieted. The very air he breathed seemed to singe his nostrils even as he had every confidence Blendingham would handle the situation and put an end to Holt's derision without any bloodshed.

Face-to-face with the vicar now, the duke flipped Holt's cravat with his quizzing glass. He cocked his brow and glared at the vicar as though he was daft. "We all have a cross to bear, my good man."

Some were heavier than others.

Several men guffawed but not Simon. A deep-seated fear began to pound in his chest as it became clearer and clearer exactly who had betrayed them: Holt.

"Y-Yes," the vicar stammered, taking a step back. His paling face slowly began to match the color of his clerical collar. "Your association with Lord Danbury's niece begs me to address another point that many here refuse to acknowledge." He sniffled loudly, the nasally sound sickening to Simon's ears. "If you hadn't been determined to find your sister's killers, and you hadn't joined Captain Frink to do so, ultimately attacking the *Octavia*, we would not have lost Collins!"

"If the duke hadn't been on the *Striker*," Guffald shouted

angrily, "I would be as dead as Collins!"

Simon cut his gaze to Gillian, swallowing back unreasonable worry. Their eyes met and didn't waver, hers glinting with suspicion. Was she thinking the same thing he was, that Holt protested too much? He appeared to be going to extremes to ensure Nelson's Tea no longer existed.

Simon's chest tightened as Blendingham cocked his hip and faced off with Holt, who stood several inches shy of the duke's six-foot height. The duke's knuckles whitened around his gold-rimmed oval monocle, a secret device that held poison in its revolving handle. Holt was certainly in danger now, not the other way around.

"Guffald has a point," Simon said, hoping to coax a confession out of the clergyman. "If His Grace hadn't joined Frink's crew, we would also have never discovered Baron Burton's duplicity or that he had employed Captain Frink."

"Perhaps the vicar would have preferred for the ladies in his parish to continue being forced to succumb to Burton's putrid appetites," Gillian said. She reached up to pat her hair, but Simon knew the impulsive movement was more than it appeared to be. She was arming herself, extracting a deadly hairpin in case it was needed.

"If Burton's evil nature taught us anything at all, it is this," Seaton chimed in. The pirate's stare locked on Holt. "The clothes do not necessarily make the man."

"What are you implying?" Holt's mouth formed an *O*, and he directed his attention to Seaton. "How dare you disparage me, you one-eyed spawn of the devil! *I* am a man of God! Compared to you, pirate, I am a saint!"

Gillian halted mid-step. "Saint?" Her stare settled on Holt, and a strange awareness crept over her face. Simon felt it too, though he couldn't quite place the source.

"More like a man of *mis*fortune," Whitbread added, fanning the flames. "There is more at play here than agreeing to continue Nelson's Tea, Vicar."

"What more could there possibly be?" Holt asked.

Whitbread cleared his throat and cut a glance to Melville and Douglas. "What our illustrious leader has yet to disclose is that we have reason to believe Seaton was captured in Spain because someone in this room betrayed him. Three of you have good reason to do so."

Men began to glance around at one another and grumble loudly.

"And no one will leave this room," Simon said, "until we get to the bottom of it."

Holt turned on Whitbread. "You—"

"Accused us of interrogating you, Vicar. Remind us," Whitbread said, assuming a legal role that mimicked his years in court. "Whose carelessness facilitated Chester Walden's death? I distinctly remember you were the one assigned to deliver information about Wickham and Walden to the House of Lords, and Walden lost his head because of it."

"How dare you! *I-I* am not on trial here, sir." Holt's eyes turned maniacal. "This is not a courtroom."

"Of course, it isn't," Gillian agreed, her tone even. "No one is accusing you of anything, Holt. Seaton was betrayed. That fact is clear, however."

"The pirate's negligence must have given him away," Holt spat.

The accusatory looks Melville and Douglas gave Holt spoke volumes, and suddenly, Simon knew their betrayer's identity. In that moment, he was overcome with a rage he could barely contain. Holt was the mole, and there was no way in hell to escape the leviathan in the room.

80

Seven

In human guise, at length to stop
The Hero's bright meridian fame,
From Santa Trinidad's top
She takes, alas! too sure an aim.
Th' envenom'd shot deep-pierc'd his heart,
A heart disdainful of all blows
By man directed: But, what art
Can guard against infernal foes?
~ "Nauticus," *The Gentleman's Magazine*, Vol. LXXV,
November 1805

A FISSURE OF light spilled through the damask curtains, aiming an iridescent midday sunbeam at the mirror above the fireplace. The reflection fragmented the room, splitting it as equally as the accusations passed back and forth. Nothing was more frightening than a house divided, except a desperate man.

Gillian suppressed a shiver. She'd dined on fear when Lucien died, despairing a future without her husband's guidance, terrified of the steps she would have to take to go on with her life. Her past, with its complications, helped her sympathize with Holt's desire for an end to war, but that was before he mentioned being a *saint*.

The word instantly brought to mind the time she was attacked by two assassins in an alley off Clarges Street. Before she'd managed to kill one of her attackers, he'd called out to the man watching her fight for her life from the alley entrance. "Saint," he'd shouted.

She searched her mind for details, the man's height and size. But in the darkness, she'd only gotten a glimpse of his silhouette. She studied Holt's face, looking for clues to his character, hardly believing what her instincts suspected to be true. Holt was the Saint, the very man who'd sent a man to murder her.

"You are trapped, *ma chérie*," the man standing near the alley had told her as she'd fought off her attacker four years ago. Before she'd been able to chase after him, to discover who he was and why he'd sent someone to kill her, her would-be assassin had disappeared. Now, in an instant, the inflection in Holt's voice—hinting that he was hiding something—brought that frightening night back to the forefront of her thoughts.

It was him! Holt was the Saint! But if he had been one of Fouché's master spies at Drury Lane, wouldn't she have recognized him? And what, for the love of God, did he have planned now?

She had to warn the others.

"All of you must listen to reason," he continued. His voice sounded desperate as he fixated on the mantle clock, acting as peculiar as he had all afternoon. His odd behavior drew her closer. The way he fidgeted with his coat suggested nervousness. "Nothing but misery awaits if we agree to continue Nelson's Tea."

Was he threatening them? Gillian couldn't be sure.

Melville's low curse reached her ears as he jumped into the verbal fracas. "I suggest we all sit down and listen to what Danbury has to say. If you are innocent of Walden's murder,

Holt, you will not deny him this courtesy."

"Excellent advice, my lord," she agreed. "Please do be seated, Vicar."

But Holt wasn't to be pacified. He turned on Gillian, and the hair rose on the back of her neck. Desperation drove men to do unconscionable things.

She swallowed back alarm, fighting not to reveal that she recognized him at last. She reached for his arm. "May I suggest—"

"No." He snapped back his arm and shied away.

She wasn't deterred. A cornered rat would attack if provoked, but if she could manipulate him into confessing . . . "I understand your anxiety."

Holt burst into laughter. "You cannot possibly understand what I am feeling now, Baroness."

"But I do." She drew close to whisper in his ear. "You were there that night in the alley."

"What?" He stared back at her as if she'd gone mad, but the telltale tic in his jaw revealed she'd hit a nerve. "I am sure I do not know what you mean."

"Yes," she said sternly. "You do."

He cackled apprehensively. "I have always respected your uncanny memory, Baroness. But," Holt went on, "I do not recall ever being in an alley with you."

Technically, the vicar was correct, though. The man known as "the Saint" had never entered the alley, preferring not to get blood on his hands. "Perhaps I am mistaken," she said softly. "Though I do not think that I am." He was *that* man.

"You are wrong!" Holt shouted, raising a brow in indignation.

How diabolical, he was! How unrepentant!

Her heartbeat quickened, and her fingers itched to ring Holt's neck. If the vicar was the one she'd seen in the alley that night four years ago as she suspected, that meant he'd been working against them since the group's inception. But how was that possible? The very idea made her sick to her stomach.

Blendingham was soon at her side, his brows knitted with concern. "Is everything all right, Baroness?"

"Yes." Everything was falling into place. "I thank you for your concern, Your Grace." The revelation of Holt's sins weighed heavily on her as she laid her hand over the duke's. "Trust me."

"You have earned my trust a thousand times over." The duke lifted her hand and placed a kiss upon it. "There will never come a day that I do not trust you."

Holt laughed again. "I find it odd that you speak of trust, Your Grace."

Gillian bit her tongue. By confronting the duke instead of backing down—in light of her discovery—Holt did himself no favors.

"We all have secrets we do not want publicly revealed," she reminded him, a brittle bite lancing her threat.

Holt fidgeted with his cuffs, his gaze darting past her to Simon. "You are not making this easy."

No. And she wouldn't. If he had been involved in the attempt on her life, she would own that the vicar had not known her four years ago. Now, he did. Surely their friendship accounted for something? "No matter our grievances, people's lives are at stake. People you and I must help," she emphasized.

A strange, lethal fury glimmered in Holt's eyes. Normally, he was an affable man, though standoffish. Today, he was irritable, defiant, and tense, as if the weight of the world sat on his shoulders. Warning bells clanged inside her, and a shiver inched down Gillian's spine.

She pressed on. "Whatever happens, we must work together." As a leader of over eight hundred souls and an overseer of the poor, surely the pious man Holt pretended to be could understand that. "Combine our efforts and talents. *You* can make a difference in protecting *your* parish, Holt— *your* country." She looked around the room at the expectant faces of the men, several of whom moved stealthily closer. And she meant to do everything within her power to distract Holt until he could be taken unawares. "We can all make a difference by trusting Lord Danbury. You know that I do."

Like the caged rat he was, Holt's gaze flitted around the room. He clasped his elbows tightly against his side. "You are not me," he said quietly.

"No." She would never betray her country. "I am not a clergyman."

Gillian bit her lower lip and watched muscles work in Holt's jaw. Corded muscles constricted above his collar as he tested his neck, moving his head back and forth. He tightened his fists while she desired to slap sense into the unreliable man.

Simon needed to be warned, but before she could act on her instincts, Holt seemed to concede. He produced a bow. "My apologies. You have suffered my surliness most cruelly, Baroness. I am, due to my ordainment, obligated by God to perform righteous works."

"Truth? Righteousness?" Milford's brows furrowed as he lifted his cigar, glaring at them. He leaned toward a candle and lit the tobacco's end, slowly puffing out one, then two plumes of smoke in Holt's direction. "No one suggested—"

"Otherwise," Chapman finished, rising from his chair to snatch Milford's cigar. He stubbed the tobacco out in a saucer. "Not here, Milford."

Russell pushed back his chair, and the splintering sound echoed loudly about them. He walked toward the bow window and closed the damask curtains, effectively snuffing out the one bit of sunlight streaming into the room. "This bickering is getting us nowhere!"

"For once, I agree with the good doctor." Holt stretched out his arms. "*Someone* must be the voice of reason. I had intended that man to be me."

Gillian's stomach churned.

"Holt," Blendingham said, adopting an effeminate pose and balancing his quizzing glass over his eye. "I am curious."

Holt straightened, giving the duke his full attention. "About what, Your Grace?"

"Your emphatic desire to disband Nelson's Tea," Blendingham said, his tone flat. "Which begs one question." Daggers shot from his eyes. "Why is it so important to you?"

Holt sneered, his face reddening. "I am a man of God—"

"Ha!" Seaton scowled.

If only he acted like one. God had nothing to do with Holt's betrayal. And if her assumptions were correct, nothing and no one, not even Lord Guildford or Holt's connections to the Church, could save him now.

"What is wrong with you, Holt?" Simon asked, moving away from the head of the table. "You are not yourself."

Gillian's heart hammered against her ribs as Holt eyed the closed door, then slid his hands over his coat. "I am *not* afraid—"

"You should be." Seaton's false smile was a frightening sight. "We're on to you."

The claw-footed ormolu clock ticked loudly in the other-wise silent room.

Tick. Tick. Tock. Tick. Tick. Tock.

Holt jabbed his finger at the pirate, a vein prominently appearing above his knitted brows. "I did not get an innocent woman killed!"

"Nor did I!" The mere mention of Esmeralda, Captain Delgado's mistress who was murdered before Seaton's eyes for passing counterintelligence to him, put the viscount on the offensive. He slammed his fist down on the table, shattering a plate. "*Someone* told Delgado where I would be! And that *someone* was *you!*"

"Liar!" Holt stiffened. "Your vile accusations disgust me, sir."

"*Lord* Seaton to you," Seaton corrected sharply.

Holt's face reddened. "More like a one-eyed devil." He looked past Gillian to Simon. "Your refusal to disband Nelson's Tea has condemned us all, Lord Danbury."

"Control yourself, Vicar," Guffald warned.

"Oh, I am past that, Captain. Danbury risked everything, including my soul, by employing these men!" Holt spat. "Look at him," he raged as Seaton drew near. He reached across the table and swiped the eye patch off Seaton's face, making Seaton howl like a demon possessed. "He's no good to us in the condition he's in now. Wherever he goes, he will draw unwanted attention. How can he effectively evade Fouché's men?"

"I will do whatever it takes!" Seaton roared, his face distorting. "I almost died for Nelson's Tea!"

"But you didn't!" Holt shouted, as if that were Seaton's true crime.

What game is Holt playing now?

Lord Seaton vaulted over the table, toppling candelabras, bowls of fruit, and crunching glass in his wake.

"No, Seaton!" But Gillian's warning was too late, and it fell on deaf ears. She tried to ward off Seaton, but Holt grabbed her by the arm and pulled her toward him. She elbowed his chest and stomped on his instep before Seaton swept her aside.

"Get back," the pirate shouted as he grabbed Holt by the collar, snatching the vicar away from her.

Gillian caught a glimpse of Simon out of the corner of her

eye. He was moving toward the unfolding melee in response to Holt provoking Seaton. Was this part of a grander plan?

Seaton's fists met Holt's flesh, creating a sickening thud. Violence solved nothing! If Holt was mortally injured, how would they ever confirm he was the one who had betrayed them? She couldn't allow this bloodletting to continue.

Gillian decided to intervene, but before she could reach the two men, strong fingers tightened around her wrist, pulling her away. She turned, ready to scold whoever had dared to stop her, and the angry retort died on her lips. It was Simon.

"You know better than to get between two fighting dogs," he told her.

"Then"—her gaze darted to the vase on the sideboard beside her—"it's a dousing they need. We cannot let this chance go."

"What do you mean—"

She wrenched her arm free and dashed for a vase. But by the time she grasped the container and turned around, the fight had already come to an end.

Seaton towered over Holt, breathing heavily, his fist primed to strike again. He glanced at the vase in her hands, the gnarly mass of flesh that had once given him sight a visible reminder of how much he'd suffered.

Anguish flooded Gillian. She lowered her makeshift weapon as the vicar struggled to rise from the Turkish carpet, then staggered to his feet. He wiped blood from his mouth, grumbled something unintelligible, then reached into his waistcoat. Something metallic glinted in the candlelight as it poked out of his pocket, but then his hand covered it completely. He started to pull his hand out of his waistcoat.

Gillian dropped the vase, ignoring the loud crash as the porcelain broke into pieces at her feet. "Look out!"

Holt snarled. Seaton lurched for the vicar's arm. The

smaller man struck Seaton's blind side, however, knocking Seaton's hulking form off-balance. Holt withdrew a pistol and spun around, aiming the barrel at Simon.

Good God, no! Instinctively, Gillian stepped in front of Simon. He reacted quickly and attempted to push her away, but she spun around to face him just as a loud *bang* echoed in the room.

Gut-ripping pain exploded in her hip as her legs went numb. Struggling to remain conscious, she collapsed into Simon, the force from the lead ball sending her tumbling into him.

Simon shouted her name, his voice raw and panicked. The others followed suit, calling out, "Baroness!" But all she could think about was the cold sweeping over her and how it contrasted the warm liquid trickling down her leg.

"My lady," Goodayle wailed.

"It's him . . ." she managed to say before she collapsed.

"No!" Simon gasped, pressing his hand to her side. Their gazes met, and dizziness and nausea washed over her. She focused on his face and the tenderness radiating there. The musk of life and the scent of death became one with her, and as she fought with all the strength she possessed to stay alive, she felt herself slipping away.

"Gillian?" Simon's lips pinched together. "Gillian, don't leave me."

A rich, heavy haze blanketed her as she opened her mouth to speak. But her throat seized and no words would come. Tears just welled in her eyes as she succumbed to d

THE AIR RUSHED out of Simon's lungs, and a pall of dread hung over him as he watched the color leach from Gillian's

face. Fear ate away at his sanity. Shouts filled the room and Holt was detained. But none of that mattered now. All he could think of was Gillian and the blood—her blood—oozing between his fingers. Terrified she would bleed out before they had time to bind her wounds, he untied his cravat, yanked it from his neck, and then pressed it to her side to staunch the flow of blood.

My darling, I cannot lose you.

No matter what he'd done to protect the woman he loved—rescuing her from her brutal father, arranging her marriage to Lucien, allowing her to live in Number Eleven, working side by side to protect England's shores—he hadn't been able to protect her when the moment called for it. *She* had protected *him*!

"Stay with me." He stroked her hair, whispering her name over and over again, kissing her tear-stained face. "Please stay with me, my love."

Russell bolted forward and dropped to a knee beside him. "Is she—"

"No," Simon cut the doctor off. He gently released her, lowering her to the carpet as if she were made of glass. "Do what you must. Just don't let her die." Their gazes locked. They both knew Simon was entrusting him with her life.

The doctor nodded. "She is in good hands, my lord. I will do everything I can."

"Do not disappoint me." The truth was, no one could disappoint him any more than he'd disappointed himself. He glanced down at his hands, shocked by the way Gillian's blood clung to his skin, feeling his reason for being alive fade with each drop spent. She'd never failed him. Even when he'd promised his life to another, she'd loved him still. And now Holt may have stolen that hard-won affection away from him.

He glanced over his shoulder, singling Holt out, prepared to rip him to pieces.

"Go," Russell prodded. "I'll take care of the baroness."

Simon curled his fingers into fists. Holt would pay for what he'd done. But not until Simon found out who was pulling the vicar's marionette strings.

He left Gillian in Russell's care and approached the circle of men, pushing several aside to reach the middle of the group where Holt was standing. He took a crushing blow to the jaw and staggered, blood trickling down his chin.

Seaton raised his fists to hit Holt again. "You sniveling coward!" he roared.

"Stop!" Simon motioned to Guffald. They needed Holt alive. The vicar was no use to them dead, as much as Simon would love to do the deed himself. Corpses could not divulge secrets, and the only one capable of calming Seaton down when he got into one of his fits of rage was the pirate's brother-in-law. "Control him!" Simon ordered Guffald.

The captain nodded and caught Seaton's fist midair. "That's enough, Seaton."

"But he shot the baroness," Seaton argued. He wrenched his hand free from Guffald's grasp and wrapped his fingers around Holt's throat. "I do not have an eye because of you! You betrayed me . . . betrayed all of us!"

Garbled sounds escaped the vicar's mouth.

"Get the vicar," Simon shouted to Blendingham. "Until we can interrogate him, we have no way of knowing what else he may have done. We need proof. Without Holt, we won't get it." Simon ran his hands through his hair. He was cast down, confounded that he'd missed signs that the clergyman had gone rogue.

Blendingham's eyes turned lethal as he strode toward Seaton. "Let him go, Captain."

"No," Seaton said with an animalistic growl. "He's in league with the devil."

The duke widened his stance, his smile cold and cruel.

"Then we must discover how deep the baptismal fount goes, eh?"

Seaton blinked, then hit Holt one more time. The vicar landed on the floor and hit his head. He moaned and shied away from the pirate, slithering like the snake that he was, in an attempt to get away.

Pathetic excuse of a man, Simon thought, thankful Nelson wasn't here to see this. *Prove you are in no hurry,* Nelson had once said, *not dictated by fear, no apprehension of the fate of this day.*

"Take him into the tunnel for interrogation," Simon said, looking to several of the men.

Blendingham nodded. "It will be my pleasure."

Confident he could entrust Holt to the duke, he returned to Gillian, who still lay unconscious before Russell.

Guilt shrouded Simon. "How is she?" he asked as Russell put pressure on the weeping wound that was bathing her silver gown red.

"The bullet went into her hip, my lord. It's still lodged there and will have to come out."

Melville strode forward, holding a handkerchief up to his nose. "La, she's bleeding everywhere, Danbury. Quick. Get her upstairs before the neighbors come pounding on the door."

"Goodayle will handle any inquiries." Simon glanced at the doorway where Goodayle stood. His eyes blazed with the fire of hell, and his face was almost as white as the sheets on a newly turned-out ship as Blendingham ordered Clemmons, Stanley, Milford, Forsyth, and Chapman to escort the struggling clergyman through the doorway and to the interrogation room.

"You cannot do this to me," Holt shouted.

"I cannot be seen here," Melville rushed out next. He was right: things were not going well for him at the Admiralty. "I cannot stay. But I also cannot, in good conscience, leave until I know the baroness is going to make it. Will she?"

Russell peered sideways at Simon. "I cannot lie. This is serious."

"Yes," Simon answered for Russell. "She will." In Simon's mind, there was no other alternative.

Seaton shoved his way through the group. "You cannot let her die."

"Don't be absurd," Melville replied, stopping Seaton in his tracks. "Russell is highly esteemed, even more methodical than his father was." He handed Seaton the eye patch he'd retrieved from the floor. "You, of all people, should know that, Seaton."

"Forgive me." Seaton grabbed the black fabric Melville handed him and yanked it into place. He nodded to Russell and Melville. "I—"

"You have nothing to be forgiven for," Simon assured him. "Escort Melville and Douglas out through the tunnels. Given the tide of recent events and the investigation into Melville's former treasury service, they might have him under close surveillance." Someone was accusing Melville of misappropriating funds, which was what initially had encouraged Melville to scour Nelson's Tea's books for discrepancies. "Either way, we cannot take the chance he's seen leaving here."

Seaton wiped his bloody nose on his sleeve, then leaned on his cane, his battered knuckles contrasting the silver nob. He nodded for Melville to make his way out of the dining room to the study. There, Seaton's men would help him exit the townhouse through a secret tunnel hidden behind a bookcase.

"Inform me as soon as you have any word about the baroness's condition," Melville said. He aimed a finger at his account books, and Douglas quickly gathered them up to follow him.

"Of course," Simon said, allowing his gaze to trail back to Gillian. "And Seaton?"

The viscount turned back to look at him. "Yes?"

"After you and your men have seen to Melville's safety, you must sail to Spain."

Seaton staggered slightly, reacting as if he'd just been slapped. "Spain?" His throat bobbed.

"I understand how hard this must be for you," Simon said, "but the Vasquez family still has the information we need. That puts them in danger. And"—*if anything motivates the viscount, it's this*—"those bloody Spaniards still have your ship. I am giving you the opportunity to get it back. That's what you want, isn't it?"

The man's countenance changed, his good eye narrowing, muscles flexing in his jaw as he studied Simon. "Aye, more than life itself."

"Take Randall and Moore."

He grinned wickedly. "I'll take my brothers, too." He motioned to Randall and Moore, and the large group headed for the tunnels.

Hungry maggots feasted on his insecurity as he watched the group follow Goodayle out of the dining room. Then he knelt down and lifted Gillian into his arms. Her body had grown colder in the few minutes they'd been apart. Fear knotted inside him as he cradled her to his chest, rendering him powerless to speak.

"Quickly," Russell commanded. "Carry the baroness upstairs as fast as you can."

Worry nursed him in a raging torrent. He nodded and took one more look at her pale features. Never before had she looked so delicate or felt so fragile in his arms. "Let's go."

Russell nodded, and Simon fell into step behind him, carrying Gillian up two flights of stairs to her bedchamber, barely cognizant that he was being followed. The good doctor opened the door wide, then stepped aside, allowing Simon space to enter. He moved swiftly and laid Gillian gently on the bed. The counterpane quickly stained crimson. His stomach recoiled as the sanctuary where their bodies had been intertwined in bliss became baptized in Gillian's blood.

Though they'd shared a love so intense it could not be extinguished by marriages to other people, they'd had too little time together.

"Step aside, my lord," Russell ordered, shouldering him out of the way when he froze, staring down at the scene before him.

Misery snapped his fragile control. "I will not leave her."

Bright sunlight shone in through the open shutters, illuminating Gillian's deathly pallor. His heart, which had been brought to life by Gillian's love, hardened into ice.

"We know you love her, Danbury." Blendingham suddenly appeared at his side and laid a hand on his shoulder.

Filled with raw emotion that had no outlet, Simon snapped his head around to look at the duke. "Why aren't you with Holt?"

"He's being handled," the duke assured him, his quiet, steadfast voice breaking through Simon's grief. "My men will take care of the vicar until I return. But you must give the doctor room to work."

Deadly calm settled over Simon as he met Blendingham's stare. "I shall kill the next man who suggests I leave her."

"Move over there, then," Russell ordered as he hurried to the other side of the bed.

Gillian's maids, Cora and Daisy, fluttered into the bedchamber like busy bees. Daisy took one look at Gillian and gasped, clutching her apron to her mouth. "What can we do, m'lord?"

"I need hot water and clean bandages," Russell demanded. "And quickly!"

A feverish need to do something meaningful burned into Simon's brain as Russell tore Gillian's gown from waist to hip, revealing the entirety of her wound. The sight of her life force seeping from her body shocked Simon into submission. Russell said something to him, but Simon couldn't hear.

Blendingham stepped forward. Guffald, who'd also followed them upstairs, did the same. "Give us a task, Russell," the duke requested.

The two men had addressed wounds like this in battle before, so Russell quickly began ordering them about. As they aided the good doctor, they fired questions back and forth, making conjectures about the depth of Holt's depravity.

"What if Lord Seaton was right? What if Holt had betrayed him—us?" Guffald asked. "His argument was sound."

Blendingham held Gillian's arms as Russell examined her wound. "That would mean he's been working with Fouché for the past *four years*. Holt's forays to Spain offered him plenty of time to coordinate Seaton's capture, which means Vasquez's family could be in immediate danger."

"That is why," Simon said, "I sent Seaton and his men back to Spain."

"None of this is circumstantial." The duke leaned closer. "Have you considered Holt worked closely with Cavendish and Walden? He arranged their travel to and from assignments, assuring the men sanctuary in churches along those routes. Is Whitbread right? Is he responsible for their deaths? Their bodies were found abandoned on the streets in Langbourne Ward. And need I mention Burton attended St. Dionis Backchurch." Blendingham growled at the mention of the baron's name. "If I find out Holt was Burton's go-between and responsible in any way for the attack on the *Octavia* and Captain Frink kidnapping my wife, I'll make sure he's dead as a nit when all is said and done."

"Have you forgotten I nearly lost my niece on the *Octavia*?" Simon didn't like being reminded of that incident, nor the moment Constance had been kidnapped from Madame Bernard's modiste shop. "I desire vengeance, too." Simon shook his head to clear his thoughts. His mind was cluttered with fear and anguish. "I am to blame as much as Holt," he said, guilt consuming him as fast as the angry sea engulfed the shore. "I recruited him. He did these things because of me."

Guffald rose to his defense. "No, my lord."

"Go," Russell ordered, shooing them away. "Quit your arguing! The lot of you! I cannot hear myself think. And I no longer need your help."

Russell's demand punched through Simon's shock, but it was the soft moan escaping Gillian's lips that cracked his composure.

"If I don't get this bullet out of the baroness now—" Russell leaned close to her chest and listened to her breathe "—she will bleed to death."

"If Gillian doesn't survive—" Devastation filled him, and he was unable to finish.

"Out!" Russell shouted. "Go somewhere else to plot and scheme. It's my responsibility to save the baroness's life, and I cannot concentrate with you here. Daisy and Cora will assist me."

"We shall do our best, Doctor." Cora, who'd quietly stayed off to the side until now, brushed past Simon to nurse Gillian.

Blendingham's face was ashen with grief as he joined Simon. He laid his hand on Simon's shoulder. "Come along, Danbury."

Daisy reentered the room, her arms laden with clean linens. Several servants filed into the room behind her, hauling in buckets of hot water.

"She will pull through, Danbury," the duke reassured

him. "I believe it, wholeheartedly. Russell has saved each of us at some point, and besides, Holt was not after the baroness."

"No. He was after me," he said. "She put herself in the line of fire for me."

"Something we all would have done had we been able," Guffald added.

"Then do not let her sacrifice be for naught," Russell scolded, looking up from Gillian's wound. "Take care of Holt, Danbury."

"Russell is right. Come, my lord." Guffald stretched out his hand. "You are compromised, and we must learn all we can from the vicar so that this does not happen again."

"Yes," Simon pledged with savage intensity. He would make Holt suffer, but only after he got the man's secrets and could make sure he never hurt anyone again.

Eight

What tho' nor friends nor kindred dear,

To grace his obsequies, attend?

His comrades are his brothers here,

And ev'ry hero is his friend!

~ "The Muffled Drum," John Mayne, *The Gentleman's Magazine*, Vol. LXXV, July 1805

SEVERAL GRUELING HOURS later, Simon was still watching the rise and fall of Gillian's chest, monitoring each shallow breath she took. Sweat beaded on his forehead and anger roiled inside him at what Holt had done to the woman Simon loved. Gillian didn't deserve this. No one did. And that was the worst part: she'd been their greatest alliance, and he loved her more than life itself, even more than the safekeeping of the king. She anchored him to logic, to hope, and to life. And for all that, he'd failed her. Here she lay, helpless before him—*because of* him.

Her dark hair, which she normally wore pulled back from her face, appeared too tight against her pale, dull, and drawn skin. Those all-seeing eyes that he desired to gaze into once more were eclipsed by coal-black lashes, featherlight guardians denying him access to her thoughts. Occasionally she grimaced, emitting the kind of pain-induced moan that shook him to his core.

How he wished he could trade places with her. It should be him lying there, not her. Never her!

A wooden drawer closed, reminding Simon that he wasn't alone. Russell was waiting for any change in Gillian's condition, having explained that the first twenty-four hours were the most critical. Cora, her devoted maid, kept vigilant watch.

"She should rest easier now," Russell said.

Cora raised a hand to her throat. "Thank the good Lord!"

"But will she recover?" Simon stroked a lock of hair away from Gillian's clammy forehead.

"That depends on the baroness. Her vitality and spirit have much to recommend her. I have always admired that about her." After a lengthy pause, Russell met Simon's eyes. "My lord, please enlighten me. What would possess Holt to try to kill you?"

Simon shrugged. "With Nelson gone, and with Holt's suggestion to disband Nelson's Tea being met with such disdain, I can only suspect that killing me was his way of fracturing the group, especially if Holt is being blackmailed into betraying us."

"But why?" Russell insisted, as if he couldn't understand. "Who would do such a thing?"

"Why does any man do what he does? A desire for power, seduction, and the promise of money—myriad reasons can always be found if you know where to look." His own participation in espionage was a journey into discovering that very thing. Why did men turn rogue? "I expect we'll find out Holt's reasons as soon as Blendingham and Guffald are done interrogating him."

But one gut-wrenching fact remained: nothing he could do, nothing he could learn from Holt, not even Holt's death, would make a difference to Gillian now. Still, the information his men acquired from the vicar would aid them in their future endeavors. It was better to know one's enemy than to be caught by surprise.

Russell nodded and looked down at his hands, still stained with Gillian's blood. "Cora, please see to it that these are cleaned well." He tossed bloody cloths to where the maid stood at the end of the bed. She caught them deftly and nodded. It was a ritual they'd perfected in the many hours they'd fought for Gillian's life together thus far.

"Aye, sir." Cora curtseyed and turned to leave the room.

"And Cora," Russell added, stopping her. "You have been a godsend. Thank you."

Cora smiled appreciatively before disappearing out the door. Russell motioned for Simon to rise, then reached past him to straighten the fresh counterpane, tucking it in around Gillian's legs. Simon felt useless, helpless, set adrift by events he couldn't control.

"She's a strong woman, my lord. The baroness has been through worse. You've seen it yourself. She will overcome her injuries. Her heart is strong and—" Russell lowered his voice "—she has much to live for." He inspected his bloody fingernails once more and frowned.

Simon took a shaky step back before gazing at his own hands. They, too, were covered in Gillian's blood still; he hadn't taken the time to wash them.

"She. Will. Live." The three words his eager heart craved to hear left Russell's mouth in a rush. His prognosis, however, did not assuage Simon's anxiety.

"And yet I get the impression you are hiding something from me, Doctor. I know you. Or have you forgotten that we have been in situations like this before, waiting for a member of our group to recover and holding back information from loved ones." He swallowed the hard lump in his throat and suppressed a shudder.

The doctor purposefully turned away, Simon supposed as

a way of avoiding eye contact, as he began to wash his hands in a floral basin set on a washstand in the corner. He took a deep breath, then spoke over his shoulder. "Exactly how close has your relationship with the baroness become?"

Irritation and something else—terror—burned hot in his throat. Why did that matter now? "We love each other."

Water sloshed in the porcelain bowl as Russell scrubbed his fingers. Simon was close to losing his mind as he waited for the doctor to pick up a towel and dry his hands.

"The bullet narrowly missed a major artery in her pelvis," Russell said.

Simon breathed a sigh of relief for Gillian's good fortune. But Russell wasn't done; that was not something he would keep secret, making Simon want to bargain, steal, do *anything* to keep from hearing what the doctor said next.

His throat burned as he asked, "Was there any other significant damage?"

Russell cleared his throat rather forcefully. "Given your late wife's struggle to provide you an heir, I feel it's my duty to inform you that Gillian will likely never conceive a child."

No children? While he would never encourage a woman to have his child after what he and Edwina had endured, he knew that Gillian desired children. A hard knot formed in the pit of his stomach, and his voice caught as he spoke. "C-Could you be wrong?"

Russell nodded unconvincingly. "Mistakes are possible in my line of work, my lord."

Simon leaned into the footboard for support. Russell's prognosis filled him with unease. He tried to process what this news would do to Gillian. "Miracles do happen. We've witnessed them before."

"You and I are realists, my lord," Russell said, folding the towel neatly, then placing it on the sideboard. "What would you have me do? Lie to her when she regains consciousness?"

"No," Simon said softly. A lie often proved worse than the secret it concealed. "Not about something like this."

Russell's medical diagnosis didn't alter his love for Gillian in any way, but he had no idea what Gillian would do when she learned the truth. Anchors moored his shoulders. She had to survive her injuries first, and if discovering that she might not be able to bear children caused her decline, he would rather she never knew.

Muscles worked in his jaw. "This is Holt's fault."

"Yes. And determining his reasons for it must be our primary focus, remember." Russell stepped toward a chair and lifted his coat from the spindly wooden backrest. He whipped the fabric around his shoulders and began shoving his right arm through a sleeve.

"Where are you going?" Simon asked, his heart sinking in his chest.

"I have another patient to see."

"But Gillian needs you!"

"Do not worry about the baroness," he said. "She is stable, and Cora and Daisy can take care of her. What do you plan to do until I get back?"

The need for vengeance coursed through Simon's veins, and no one was safe. "Find out why Holt betrayed us."

"And afterward?" Russell asked.

"I'll ensure he never hurts anyone again," he said with lethal finality.

"No!" Gillian cried out, thrashing violently as if struggling to speak had cost her everything.

They rushed to her side. Sweat beaded on her brow as another feverish wave appeared to sweep over her.

"Hold her still!" Russell, his coat only half-on, nearly knocked over the basin in his attempt to reach Gillian and hold her still. "She mustn't move. We have to keep her as calm and immobile as possible."

Simon held her down with one hand, then dipped a cloth in a bowl of water beside the bed. He wiped her forehead with the cool compress, whispering, "Shh, my love. You are safe. Everything is going to be fine."

Gillian seemed as if she didn't hear him and drifted back into oblivion. Fear engulfed his soul. He felt helpless and lost, crippled by doubt and the haunting memory of Gillian thriving in his arms. Her silence, the sweat beading on the motionless lips that had declared her love for him, filled him with impotent rage. He closed his eyes and grasped her hand to his forehead.

He heard Russell shrugging his coat the rest of the way on. "I will leave you now. Once the baroness's maids return, go and do what you must . . . Make whoever is to blame pay." He stood there silently, waiting for a response Simon did not give him, then left the room.

Hearing the doctor speak in such a way clashed with the stalwart man who'd sworn never to take life but protect it. His vocation as a doctor provided him access to stately homes, hospitals, and prisons, places where various members of Society congregated. Unlike Holt, who'd stolen from his flock, if Melville's and Douglas's files were any indication, Russell could be counted on. Simon felt it deep in his marrow.

As Simon reached out and touched Gillian's cheek, Cora and Daisy walked in and each bobbed a curtsy.

"Excuse our interruption, m'lord," Cora said, "but the doctor informed us that we were needed 'ere."

"Of course." He stared at Gillian a few more precious moments, memorizing the look of her and allowing her suffering to fuel the anger festering inside him. Then he rose and walked around the bed, summoning all his strength to leave the room. "Watch over her, ladies," he said. "If she wakes . . . if she is in need of anything at all, send for Goodayle. He will know where to find me."

"As ye wish, m'lord," Daisy said.

He headed for the door without looking back and closed it soundlessly behind him. He laid his forehead against the cool wooden frame on the other side. Hours of listening to Gillian cry out as Russell dug into her flesh was a cancer gnawing on his insides. He could still hear the lead ball Russell had retrieved from her hip plunking into a steel dish. Moreover, he would never forget the sheer panic in her eyes, the way she'd clung to his hand as the surgeon probed deeper inside her. Infection was their greatest enemy now.

Simon splayed his fingers on the doorframe, once more directing his gaze to his stained fingernails. *Enough!*

He turned, rounded the balustrade, and descended the stairs, each creak in the floorboards a nail pounding into Holt's coffin. His heartbeat thrummed in his throat as he swallowed back emotions threatening to override his good sense. How was he to balance the scales without knowing his true enemy, without giving away his hand?

The townhouse was eerily quiet as he stepped down on to the ground floor and moved along the corridor to the dining room. He strode in without hesitation, eager to get to the bottom of Holt's treachery. In his absence, shattered dishes and pieces of glass that had been littering the table and the Turkish carpet had been meticulously retrieved and shepherded away, leaving no proof of what had transpired hours earlier.

Simon made a circuit of the room, passing righted portraits and the gilded mirror hanging prominently above the fireplace where the ormolu clock perfectly ticked away time. Even Gillian's blood had been scrubbed from the floor. He scowled, remembering all too clearly the moment Gillian had been shot. Wrestling with his thoughts, he regarded the scene outside the bow window—carriages passing, people taking their daily walks—until he sensed he was no longer alone.

He turned toward the entrance. "Goodayle," he said. "I see you have been busy."

Goodayle dipped his head. "The servants had naught else to do."

"Of course." Simon nodded. "Ingenious of you."

"Thank you, my lord."

"And has the *vicar* received adequate attention?"

"He's below, my lord."

Goodayle would never openly challenge him, but his narrowed eyes revealed intense hatred for any mention of Albert Holt, the once-stately vicar who had blessed the four walls of Number Eleven.

"It's only a matter of time," Simon said, hinting that satisfaction would come, one way or another. "We will soon know why he tried to kill me."

The anger that blazed in Goodayle's eyes spoke of his desire to make Holt reap what he'd sown.

"Come," Simon said, moving through the room and out into the hallway.

"This is my fault." Goodayle fell into step behind him. "I have but one job, and that is to protect those within this townhouse. Perhaps if I had been more diligent, I might have—"

"You are nothing but," he reassured Goodayle as he stopped at the study doors. He spun around and placed his hand on the loyal man's shoulder. "We have been trained to presume many things, but nothing could have prepared us for this. Holt tricked us all."

"Aye, my lord," Goodayle said. The nod to their former navy life prodded Simon to believe his old friend was returning to himself again.

He patted Goodayle's shoulder. "We must discover if Holt was commissioned to infiltrate Nelson's Tea or if the vicar acted alone."

"Could he be working for the French?" Goodayle asked.

"That, my good man," he said, pointing his finger aloft, "is what I'm going to find out." He turned to leave, then stopped. He faced Goodayle again. "When Russell returns, make sure he has everything he needs at his disposal. I've instructed Cora and Daisy to fetch you if the baroness's condition worsens before I return."

"Yes, my lord." Goodayle bowed his head and then retreated down the hall.

Simon faced the scrollwork decorating the study entrance. Inhaling deeply, he gripped the door handles, stepped into the room, and then turned to quietly close each door behind him. With little effort, he gave his library a thorough once-over, noting the fire blazing in the hearth. He moved to the fireplace, which was flanked by floor-to-ceiling bookcases, and deftly grabbed the third Grecian medallion frieze from the right, moving the circular dial left one and a quarter turn. A mechanism inside the wall slipped into gear, popping one section of the bookcase outward. Simon eased it open, turned another knob, and watched the hidden aperture close before making his way into the secret passage that led to the tunnels beneath the townhouse.

"Who sent you?" Blendingham's voice drifted to Simon in the darkness, raw hatred spilling from his tongue.

Another cold voice followed. "Why have you betrayed us?" It was Guffald.

The same questions riddled Simon's brain, and his mind raced to come up with realistic—though nowhere near excusable—explanations. Melville and Douglas had arrived at the townhouse before anyone else. They had found discrepancies in the legacies left by deceased aldermen and merchants in Langbourne Ward and learned that the funds were set aside to help the poor who frequented St. Dionis Backchurch—Holt's parish. Why had the vicar stolen from his parishioners? Had someone found out? If that information had fallen into the wrong hands, Holt could have easily been blackmailed into betraying them for fear of losing all he cherished. Simon moved through the winding tunnel, silently cursing the man who'd almost murdered the love of his life.

"Answer Guffald's question," the duke shouted.

"Do what you want with me," Holt spat. "I am not afraid . . . to die."

Holt's hollow vow, and the telltale drop in his tone that implied he was lying, attracted Simon like a fly to meat. He quickly reached the door to the secluded room with its iron-barred window and opened it. The hinge grated loudly, announcing his presence. There, ten of his men filled the twenty-by-twenty-foot room.

"Should you be here?" Blendingham asked as soon as he appeared in the doorway. His white wig and fashionable attire had been discarded, and the duke rose to acknowledge Simon. His shirtsleeves were rolled up to his elbows, and drops of blood were splattered across his chest. He rubbed one of his hands, drawing attention to his bloody knuckles.

Simon ignored the man's grisly appearance; it was Holt he wanted to see.

The vicar was seated in the center of the room, struggling against his bonds. "You gave me no choice!" Blood trickled down his face to his chest. "You would not agree—"

"So you tried to kill me?" Anger tightened Simon's chest.

"We all saw it," the duke said. "We agree on that,"

"Or was it your plan all along to kill the baroness?" Simon asked, his fingers itching to wrap around Holt's throat so he could watch the life drain out of him.

The vicar forced a laugh. "I didn't—"

"No. You did not mean to betray us." He narrowed his eyes before cutting them to the duke. "No matter how much you beg, there will be no negotiations." His voice was cold and harsh as he stepped toward Holt, near enough to look right into the vicar's bruised, swollen, and guarded eyes. How far afield had Holt's treachery taken him? Simon was desperate to know. "Why?" he asked. "Who put you up to this?"

Holt licked his bloody lip. "Is she . . . dead?"

In a fit of fury, Simon backhanded Holt. The vicar's head rebounded, then sagged toward his chest. "She's alive, no thanks to you." He raised his fist to strike again. "I *want* answers," he ground out, "and I expect to get them."

"*I* will get your answers," Blendingham said. "This is what I do best. You should return to the baroness. She needs you."

"Aye," Guffald grumbled. "I say that once Blendingham has learned all we want to know, we should return the vicar to his parish."

"Allowing the wolves to move in for the kill, eh?" Blendingham grinned. "I like how you think, Captain."

"N-No!" Holt's eyes widened. They were filled with a manic plea that bore into Simon. "Do not leave me alone w-with *him*!"

Simon ignored the clergyman's pitiful outburst. The duke was right. As much as Simon wanted to interrogate Holt himself, Gillian needed him. Venom dripped from his words as he said, "Your luck has run out, Vicar."

"Kill me and be done with it," he rushed out.

"Kill you?" Blendingham asked incredulously, slapping a piece of leather against his palm. "I have no intention of killing you. Maiming you, perhaps. Ensuring you suffer unimaginable pain, drawing out your agony, sure. I do not know the particulars yet, but you are responsible in part for Guffald's and Seaton's injuries. I will discover to what degree. But killing you? No, that is not a part of *my* plan."

Blendingham looked past Simon, who turned as Clemmons and Stanley entered the room and came to stand beside the duke, followed by Winters and Edwards. Hamlet had taken up residency in the corner, where he sketched out Holt's interrogation. Chapman sat beside him, recording the scene as if he were taking minutes. At a table in another corner, Whitbread spoke quietly with Forsyth.

The latter fastened his stare on Simon. "He might be responsible for the deaths of Chauncey, Collins, Cavendish, and Walden, as well, m'lord. We're all eager to find out if 'tis true."

Forsyth's revelation didn't surprise Simon. Walden and Forsyth had grown up in Aberdeenshire, and the two Scots had been thick as thieves. So if Holt was responsible for Walden's death, Forsyth would be the man to find out.

Simon clung religiously to Nelson's code as the foundation beneath his feet.

1. *Induce the enemy, tempt him to react. Nothing is predictable.*

2. *No captain can do very wrong if he places his ship alongside that of an enemy. Flexibility saves lives.*

3. *Always be on hand to assist friends.*

4. *Maintain a degree of coolness and deliberation in forming plans of escape.*

5. *Execute with astonishing ardor and heroism.*

Every one of these men had invested blood and bone in the vice-admiral's creed. It was second nature to them now. All, except Holt.

Simon approached the vicar, his frustration mounting. They were prepared to do whatever they had to, no matter how long it took to discover the truth. "Let's begin."

"No, m'lord." Stanley marched up to Simon and saluted him. "'I wish to kill the bear that *I* might carry its skin to my father.'"

Stanley's quotation of the words Nelson had used on his first voyage at sea stirred Simon's soul. The story was impressed on their hearts and retold in times of hardship, a reminder that anything that needed to be done could be done as long as one willed it. He glanced around the room, taking stock of his determined men. And just as the vice-admiral had been given permission to disembark and hunt down a polar bear so that he could kill it, and then present its hide to his father, his men banded together now, eager to learn why Holt had deceived them and just how far the vicar had gone to do so. Justice would be found.

"Allow me to do the 'onors," Stanley pleaded. "Ye are needed elsewhere."

"That's right. Go!" He struggled against his bonds more aggressively. "Abandon your men!"

"You are not in a position to dictate orders, Vicar," Winters said, rolling onto the balls of his feet. "You are a liar and a thief. You do not deserve our compassion." He smacked his fist into his hand. "If you recall, our esteemed admiral used to say, 'Officers are born to command, seaman to obey. When this fails, there is always the cat.' As it happens, I have a cat, and I am happy to oblige."

"Please . . ." Sweat beaded on Holt's forehead. "Yes . . . Yes, I have done things, horrible things, to stay alive. I've lived beyond my means. I've stolen from the poor. I am a despicable wastling, but I've been ill-used by the men who control my fate." He licked his bloody lip. "Hear me. I never wanted to hurt anyone." He swallowed thickly. "I advised Walden not to follow me, knowing the man's curiosity would get him killed. But he did, and they murdered him."

"They?" the duke asked. "Who . . . are . . . they?"

"Demons," Holt stated matter-of-factly and with spite. "Men in league with the devil, who treasure power over righteousness and peace." His shifty eyes settled on them one at a time. "They worship the depths of their pockets, and they will ruin anyone who stands in their way. So you see, I had to obey them. They'd discovered I'd stolen from my parish, and they threatened to—"

So Simon had guessed rightly . . .

"A pitiful attempt to attain our sympathy," Guffald scolded. "I suspect you would do or say anything to keep from suffering the kind of pain you have doled out. You have admitted your guilt, and you stand convicted in God's eyes and under Nelson's law—the very doctrines you swore to uphold."

"God knows my heart," Holt confessed through cracked, swollen lips. "Nelson was a vain man, an adulterer. *You* are only men!"

"Men that hold your life in their hands." Whitbread moved swiftly toward Holt, but the duke barred his path. "We were friends!" the barrister shouted. "And there is no commandment more extraordinary, Vicar. 'Blessed is he who lays down his life for his friends.' Does that not ring true in your ears?"

"Yes," Holt groveled. "May God bless Walden's, Chauncey's, Cavendish's, and Collins's souls."

"But the baroness!" Whitbread clawed his way out of the duke's arms intent on planting Holt a facer. "She didn't deserve—"

"No. She didn't," Simon said sternly, rounding his fist and landing a punch to Holt's jaw himself.

The vicar's head wheeled, and he spat blood. "You won't get away with this. People in high places will look for me. My congregation. My fellow clergymen."

"Only God can save you now," Simon said, wiping his knuckle on Holt's sleeve, "for you are not safe from us, nor the king."

"You . . . are wrong," Holt said. "You will see. Lord Fle—" The vicar coughed in an apparent attempt to cover for his slight of tongue.

"Fleming?" Simon asked, perplexed.

Guffald laid a hand on Simon's shoulder. "We will discover what Lord Fleming has to do with this or if Holt is casting stones. If he is involved, we will get to the heart of it."

"Leave Holt to us, Danbury," Blendingham implored for a third time. "Your place is with the baroness."

Chapman, ever in the employ of the *Gazette*, put down his feathered quill. "If Lord Fleming is involved, the trail may not end there. What of Lord Guildford?"

Simon scrubbed his jaw. "He is a respectable member of the House of Lords. An investigation this size—"

"Will get you all killed." Holt trembled. "Can you not see? If you do not disband, you are signing your death warrants, and my own. They will hunt me down to the ends of the Earth. I have done things . . . and I know too much."

"Then there is only one option, Vicar. You must tell us all you know and then disappear." Chapman's suggestion echoed the sentiments in Simon's head.

"What are you suggesting?" Whitbread asked, incredulous.

"His death will surely send a message to whoever put him up to this," Blendingham said with a wave of his hand. "I, for one, would gladly see to it." He grinned wickedly at the simpering, spineless vicar.

"As would I," several men chimed in.

"No," Simon said. "We need the vicar alive if we are to have any leverage with our enemies. Because we do not know exactly who we are up against, killing him could spark a political gale of epic proportions. That is something the king will not tolerate, especially at this time. Trafalgar may be won, but Melville faces serious accusations in the House of

Lords, where it's believed he's misused millions of the Royal Navy's money, and there is still Nelson's funeral to plan. The baroness requires Russell's care, and in addition, our chief allies in Spain, the Vasquez family, are in danger." Simon contemplated Holt's fate with deadly calm. "No. There are other ways to learn what we need to know."

The duke popped his knuckles in swift fashion. "And when, I ask you, have we ever run away from a challenge, eh?"

Whether the vicar was pushed or willingly jumped, they were declaring war on the person or persons involved in Holt's fall from grace. And this road they chose would lead to unconscionable suffering for many or all of them, though they'd already suffered much.

"You cannot do this!" Holt raged when Simon finally turned to leave.

"Oh, but you are wrong there, Vicar." At Clemmons's and Stanley's nods, Blendingham moved closer. "As a peer, I answer only to my sovereign. But as a pirate, I'm at liberty to do whatever the hell I please."

Nine

See Love and Truth, all woe begone;
And beauty, drooping in the crowd—
Their thoughts intent on him alone
Who sleeps forever in his shroud!
~ "The Muffled Drum," John Mayne, *The Gentleman's Magazine*, Vol. LXXV, July 1805

"Gillian?"

She fought to open her eyes. Bright light and a familiar voice fractured the peace she'd clung to in the bleak darkness. Her thoughts, muddled as if by fog, fought back the crimson-purple shadows that haunted her awareness, choosing instead to concentrate on Simon's voice. It was an irresistible lure that awakened her senses to lavender, lemon, and a harsh metallic smell. She wrinkled her nose.

Blood. Hers.

The sound of tinkling porcelain knifed through her brain, and then the swish of a woman's skirts joined the symphony. Voices murmured softly, drawing her attention. Russell and Daisy came into focus. They stood together and peered anxiously at her. An unbidden tear slipped down her cheek at the joy of seeing them again, then excruciating pain infiltrated her senses. Gillian moaned and glanced at the ceiling, feeling adrift as other voices filled her ears, men arguing for and against disbanding Nelson's Tea. Desperation gripped her as the gunshot echoed in her memories. She clenched her jaw and choked back the sob threatening to burst from her throat as fear for Simon's safety came flooding back.

"Gillian?" Simon's face appeared, real and steadfast before her.

He is alive! She could not resist the pull he had on her soul more than she could the breath entering her lungs. But each inhale and exhale made her distinctly aware that there was a throbbing pressure in her side, and she desperately wanted to put an end to it.

Simon looked as if he'd been to battle. His cravat hung low and crooked. Raw skin around his neck indicated he'd tugged the fabric one too many times, and above his stubbly jaw, worry was etched into his face. He placed a cool compress on her forehead, then smoothed errant strands of hair away from her eyes. "You've come back to me at last."

How long . . .

His quivering voice held a torment and fatigue similar to the one he'd had when they'd sought refuge from French spies on the banks of the Thames. That mission had not ended well; several innocent bystanders had died as a result, and Simon had blamed himself.

She parted her numb, chapped lips and tried to get her thick, sluggish tongue to perform.

"Shh. Easy now, Gillian. You must take it slow."

She nodded weakly and shuddered. The vicar's angry face flashed in her mind.

"Holt!" She sprang up from the bed. "You must . . . stop him . . . Simon!"

"You needn't worry about him," he said, easing her back down to her pillow. "He's being dealt with."

That meant they were interrogating Holt or had already done so. *Blast!* For what the vicar had almost cost her, she desired to string up the man herself!

Questions swirled around in her brain. Why had Holt tried to kill Simon at all? He'd been dedicated to the Church, and such a thing was not acceptable. She tried to conjure pity for the poltroon but couldn't. He'd made his choice.

She inhaled a steadying breath and gazed into Simon's eyes. "Take me to him."

He shook his head. "You are in no condition to go anywhere."

"Take me to him," she said again. "I have been injured before."

Simon leaned back and frowned. "You cannot be serious."

"I am." And she was—deadly serious. "I want . . ." Her voice broke, and damn her, another tear slipped down her cheek. "I need to make sure the vicar cannot harm you again."

"As do I." He smiled and stroked her forehead, his voice a soft caress. "But I will never allow you to martyr yourself, least not for me."

She drew in an audible breath. "I lost you once. I cannot—" She swallowed, hard.

"Shh. You haven't lost me. I am here," he gently reminded her.

Her lungs seized as the rightness of his words sank in. "Simon, I—"

"Must get well," he cut in. "That is all you must think about right now."

She shook her head and struggled to rise, grimacing as she worked herself up on her elbows. If Holt wanted to kill Simon, there might be others.

"What are you doing?" he asked, trying to ease her back down. "You are supposed to be resting."

"There isn't time. We must make sure he cannot threaten

you again."

He stopped resisting her and allowed her to rise, even helping her to her feet. The endeavor nearly made her swoon. Pain instantly snatched at her senses, and she clutched her side. Gathering her resolve, she lifted her arms to ply the top of her hair with her fingers, rejoicing when she found the deadly hairpins she kept there. "Take me to him." She lowered her arms and brandished the sharp weapon before Simon, losing her balance.

"Ye didn't remove 'er 'airpins?" Daisy screamed and turned to Russell as Simon caught Gillian. "The baroness is clever. She 'ides weapons all over 'er person. Surely ye didn't neglect to check 'er 'air during yer examination."

"I am a doctor, not a weapons expert." Russell turned a strange shade of pink. "And I am certainly not a maid. That is your job. I had more pressing concerns at the time, Daisy."

"Enough!" Simon lifted Gillian carefully into his arms, then motioned for Daisy to join her. "Take them. I entrust them to your care."

"Of course, m'lord." Daisy clasped the hairpins to her chest. "Never ye mind about 'em, m'lady. I will see they are kept safe. Ye must concentrate on yer recovery."

"Yes," she said, fatigue settling over her. She allowed Simon to help her back onto the bed, then reclined against the pillows, wincing. But the pain stitching her side was nothing compared to the possibility that Holt—and those associated with him—would get another chance to kill Simon. Her gaze gripped his. "What has he told you?"

"Baroness." Russell stepped forward and handed her a glass of wine. "Drink this."

"You must rest," Simon insisted once more. "There is no reason for you to exhaust yourself. We are verifying Holt's confession as we speak."

How could she rest when no one knew how deep Holt's

betrayal went? Worry filled her breast, and rightly so. She had opened her heart and home to the vicar. He'd abused her generosity, her trust, as well as those in her care. Her mind was a whirl of emotion as she sought a tangible fact, image, word that he might have said to indicate his true intentions. She should have recognized the change taking place in the vicar sooner—the tension in his shoulders, his restlessness. Indeed, her observations had come too late. How could she have known his loyalties had changed?

Oh, if only she'd seen through his disguise. Perhaps then she could have spared them all his treachery. Guilt-ridden, she raised the glass to her lips and drank the bitter wine. "What did I miss?" She sighed and tried to sit up again.

"We will discuss this at a better time." Simon took the glass from her hand and gingerly pressed her back onto the pillows. "You will not do anyone good, especially yourself, if you rip out your stitches, Gillian." He smiled sadly. "The duke has Holt below. I have everything under control."

"I want—" she sighed again and licked her lips, feeling the pain ease from her body "—to see for myself."

"What is wrong?" Simon gently prodded. He cupped both sides of her face and searched her eyes. "Are you in pain?"

She tried to ease his mind by shaking her head, but it was difficult to do so while Simon held it between his hands. Simon's brows knit together, and then he looked away. "Is there nothing more you can do for her, Russell? I do not want Gillian ingesting laudanum. My late wife—"

"No need to explain, my lord," Russell said. "I am well aware of what happened to your wife. I have given the baroness a tonic of saffron. It will not harm her."

Simon's throat constricted, and her heart tugged at the emotion he displayed. "I cannot watch the woman I love suffer like that again."

"And damned if I do not know it." She'd rarely heard the

doctor use that abrasive tone before. No doubt, this wasn't the first time Simon had confronted him in such a way. "I cannot bring myself to think what—"

"Do not quarrel," she said, craning her neck to see Russell and Daisy more clearly. She cut her gaze to Simon and grabbed his hand. "Did I hear you say . . . the duke is with Holt?"

He nodded assuringly. "Yes."

"And Guffald? Where is he?"

"He is helping the duke. Most of the men are."

"Seaton, too?" she said hopefully.

Simon blinked. He shifted positions, a sign her question unnerved him, and then he cleared his throat. "I . . . sent him to Spain."

A fresh wave of nausea and panic swept over her. Her breath hitched. "Spain?"

"It could not be helped, my love," Simon explained. "Our informants are at risk and Seaton has unfinished business there."

She knew what kind. D'Auvergne had written that the *Priory* was still docked at a port in San Sebastian. "His ship."

"Yes. And Holt just confirmed that Lydia is in trouble."

Lydia Vasquez was Constance's aunt. Years ago, Simon had introduced the former Lady Lydia Claremont to Don Alberto Vasquez, and the two had married, uniting to monitor Napoleon's activities.

"Lady Vasquez?" She placed trembling fingers on her throbbing temples as the concoction Russell had given her slipped over her like a fine, kid leather glove. She bit her lower lip, not knowing if she'd draw blood. God's teeth! Would the viscount return with his sanity intact? Or return at all? "How could you . . . send him *there*?"

Simon didn't flinch. "I acted on the Vasquez's behalf. Seaton is the only one capable of getting into San Sebastian without detection. He speaks the language; his father has contacts there, and no one will expect him to return after all he's been through."

The seriousness of the situation reflected in Simon's eyes. "There are others just as capable," she reminded him, including Seaton's sister. "Send Lady Adele and . . . Guffald. They can do this."

"Guffald is helping the duke."

She blinked back her drowsiness and fought to stay focused. "You have sent him back to hell."

Russell cleared his throat as Simon's shoulders sagged. "Nothing more can be done. Seaton has already left."

"Nothing . . . better happen to him," she warned.

"Shh, now," Simon cooed. "Leave Seaton to me. He is stronger than you think. You must concentrate on getting well."

"What I think—" she glanced around the room sleepily "—does not . . . appear to matter."

Simon's face pinched. "Everything about you matters to me."

Russell cleared his throat again. "It's time to leave, Daisy." He motioned for her to accompany him. "Come along."

Daisy moved noiselessly around the bedchamber, gathering Gillian's discarded clothes. When she finished, her forlorn gaze settled on Gillian, her apprehension to do as she was told touching Gillian deeply. "I never dreamed ye'd come to 'arm 'ere, m'lady." She dabbed a tear streaming from the corner of her eye. "If ye 'ave need of me, I'll be down the 'all. All ye 'ave to do is call me name."

"Thank you," she said and reached out her hand.

Daisy grasped Gillian's hand with both of her own and smiled warmly. She raised Gillian's hand to her lips, her inner torment all too visible in her red-rimmed eyes. Then she set Gillian's hand gently back on the bed, bobbed a curtsy, and followed Russell out of the room.

Gillian waited for Simon to speak.

He tested her forehead with the back of his hand. "Are you in pain?" he asked, caressing her face.

"'Tis nothing," she said, trying to ease his worry. Truth be told, the saffron tincture had eased all sensation.

"We are alone now. Tell me the truth." Simon's gray eyes softened around the edges, and his voice comforted her in a silken embrace. "How do you feel?"

She took inventory of her body, testing her fingers and toes with a wiggle. Then she shifted her left knee, and a sharp tug traveled through her right side. Lowering her head, she glanced down at the counterpane.

"How badly am I injured?" she asked. The vicar's attempt to kill Simon still shocked her to her core.

"You are lucky to be alive," he said, raking his hand through his hair. "The bullet barely missed a major artery."

Similar to Guffald's latest wound, she thought. Would she be plagued by a limp now, as well? Tears welled in the backs of her eyes, but she refused to let them fall now. She'd been injured before—countless times, in fact. Why did this time feel so . . . final?

"There is something"—she glanced away, unable to meet his eyes—"you and Russell are not telling me, isn't there?"

Simon's face went grim. "Bad news and good news, I am afraid."

"Related to . . . the surgery?" she asked.

He shook his head. "To the path the bullet took in your body."

"Tell me," she said, her voice barely above a whisper.

"Gillian." His throat bobbed strangely, as if he couldn't get enough air. "Russell said it is unlikely you will ever be able to . . . carry a child."

His words broke through her haze. She clutched Simon's

arm. "No children?" She let out a pent-up breath.

"I am sorry, my love." His voice broke.

No children . . .

She and Lucien had never had a child, and truthfully, she wasn't quite sure how two spies would raise children together. Over their five-year marriage, she'd assumed she was barren, as much as she would have gladly borne Lucien a child. There was a small hope in her, though, that one day she'd be able to give Simon the child he and Edwina could not have, either. She was still young, just twenty-seven. Surely . . . She tried to take a steadying breath. It was no use pondering that kind of life now. Like Simon, then Lucien and Lord Nelson, this too had been stolen from her.

She fought the effects of the saffron, her heart breaking for Simon as she gazed into his eyes, fearing what this loss would cost him. She couldn't survive losing him a second time. She blinked back tears. "Holt did this . . . to us."

His mouth turned downward. He squeezed her hand and nodded coolly. "Yes." A heartbreaking ache unlike any she'd ever known gripped her. "You almost died," he said.

She reached out her hand and stroked his cheek. "Simon . . ."

"You promised you'd never put your own safety at risk for me, Gillian."

"I have promised you many things throughout the years." Her voice quivered. "Once . . . or twice."

"You should never have put yourself in harm's way," he exclaimed.

"I *couldn't* help it, my lord." She laughed, the irony biting into her brain. Her actions had taken away the one thing they had hoped to someday share—a family. And yet, given another chance, Gillian knew she would do exactly the same thing to save Simon's life. She grasped his hand and placed it over her heart, feeling a familiar ache in her breast. "*You* are my life."

He didn't speak but watched her silently. Then without removing his hand, he unexpectedly shifted to lie on the bed next to her, propping his head up on the adjoining pillow with his other hand.

"This is . . . improper," she said, despite how much she enjoyed his nearness. "What if . . . Russell walks in?"

"*This* is where I belong," he said. "I am an extension of your heartbeat."

A tear slipped down her cheek unheeded. She had struggled long and hard to stake a claim on this gentle rogue. She removed her hand from his and touched Simon's chest.

He closed the distance between them and leaned his forehead against hers. Simon was alive and safe; she'd succeeded in shielding him. That alone made everything she'd sacrificed worthwhile. And yet, a piece of her felt missing. The dam burst, and her tears began to fall.

Simon held her while she cried. "I do not care whether or not we have children. That has no effect on the way I feel about you. I just want to be with you, Gillian." His words flowed over her like honey, a welcome, soothing balm to her soul. "I love you."

Her heart clenched. "I love you, too."

He tilted his head back, and his smoldering stare intensified as he gazed into her eyes. "Marry me," he said.

Gillian's heart felt as if it would burst, but it would be sheer lunacy to agree. Guilt plagued her. He'd married another woman based on his father's desire for an heir, and now Gillian's desperation to save his life could have stolen the possibility of her ever having a child, their child. Could he truly forgive her that? Truly be happy without a child of their own?

He wasn't deterred, whispering, "Will you marry me, my sweet love?"

"Simon . . ." Her breath caught. Fresh tears welled in her eyes. It felt as if she'd waited a lifetime to hear him say those four words, but was he merely motivated by the moment? She peered at him through her lashes, fearing the undeniable feeling of rightness arrowing through her. She loved him passionately. His father, her past, their enemies, even Holt could not breach that bond. But her inability to give him a child *could*.

"I cannot bear your silence," he said, a subtle hitch of insecurity in his voice.

She closed her eyes, fighting back the murky, medicinal fog that continued to creep over her thoughts. "What about Nelson's Tea?"

"We can lead the group together."

"What about . . . the *ton*?" she asked, her tongue thickening.

He grumbled. "I care nothing about the *ton*."

"Your brother does."

"Rock," he said, using his brother's nickname, "will not come between us. I will never allow anyone that power again." He caressed her cheek, lulling her into a state of completeness. His eyes darkened. "Do you hold Seaton's journey to Spain against me?"

"No." Tears filled her eyes, and she fought back horrific images of the viscount having been tormented and abused. Would Seaton survive another encounter with Spaniards?

"Have you fallen out of love with me so quickly, then?" Simon asked.

"N-Never." She inhaled his masculine scent, longing to be at his side until the end of her days. "You are the air that I b-breathe."

His heartbeat sped beneath her touch. "Then agree to be my wife."

She yearned to give in but struggled to stay focused as her

mind and heart protested. He deserved a woman who could give him much more than companionship, who could give him a family. "This is—"

"Just say *yes*," he said, his voice buoyed by hope. "Make me the happiest of men."

She summoned her iron will. "What if—"

"Nothing is assured. You know this better than I do. Marry me, Gillian."

Gooseflesh prickled her skin as Simon clasped her slender fingers between his and raised them to his lips. He kissed them tenderly. Warmth exploded within her, and she fought back more tears. Love was such an all-consuming emotion, and it swept over her in a wave of endless joy. Speechless, she laid her head on Simon's shoulder and breathed in his leather-and-spice scent, feeling weightless and cherished in his arms as the potion Russell had given her magically syphoned her strength.

"If you will not answer me, my lady, I shall make it my life's mission to convince you."

"You are relentless," she teased. "And I love you for it."

"Then say the words I want to hear. Tell me you will marry me."

"I do want to marry you." She sighed contentedly. "With all my heart." Her body felt heavy and warm, and his nearness offered the kind of comfort she could only find in Simon's arms. "Yes," she said, finally yielding. "I will . . . marry you."

He shifted on the bed, then encircled her hand with his and placed something on her finger. His voice was like a soft caress. "It's settled. We will be married as soon as you recover."

"I shall do my best," she replied.

He kissed her lips. "I will hold you to that promise."

Ten

Britain has felt three losses most severe:
NELSON, her hero on the boundless main,
The constant scourge and dread of France and Spain;
CORNWALLIS, India's fav'rite—Ireland's friend,
Wise to conciliate, valiant to defend;
And PITT, the dauntless pilot of the State,
By birth, in talents, eminently great.
These have, alas! now pass'd that awful bourn
Whence Fate's decree for ever bars return!
~ "The Triple Loss," Thomas Stott, *The Gentleman's Magazine*, Vol. LXXVI, February 1806

As THE DAYS passed, Gillian's health improved. So did Simon's disposition as he set about dedicating himself to discovering the source of Holt's fall from grace. Blendingham and Guffald had stayed on hand to assist him while other members of Nelson's Tea had been sent on clandestine errands, spying on the men Holt had implicated, namely Lord Fleming. For the time being, they'd sequestered the vicar in the tunnels below the townhouse for the man's own protection.

An impassioned debate among the members of Nelson's Tea had preceded that action. Votes had been cast with many members demanding Holt's head on a platter. Some argued that their betrayer should be transported to the Admiralty and placed in a cell to rot for all time, but Blendingham, the good and meticulous man that he was, reminded them all what had happened when Captain Frink had been incarcerated in Whitehall. Through connections unbeknownst to them, he had escaped.

All eyes had fallen on Guffald then, for he'd acquired his limp after Frink's escape, when he had been gunned down trying to protect Blendingham's wife, who was then kidnapped by Frink and his cohort, Montgomery, Baron Burton. It quickly had been decided that anyone wielding that type of influence could also acquire access to the vicar. However, Holt's death was something they could not risk, at least not yet. They needed him, as Whitbread had attested: he was an essential and influential witness who would help bring the true villains to justice.

"How long do you suppose it will take to discover the truth of this matter?" Gillian asked sweetly from the chaise longue where she rested at her leisure in the parlor. They were alone in the room, which made Simon feel more at ease as Gillian lowered the book she was reading to her lap and gave him her full attention. "Uncovering the vicar's secrets may take more time than our allies can afford."

"Yes," Simon said, "time is not something we have to spare." He stopped pacing the Turkish carpet and turned to face the woman who stole his breath every time he looked at her.

Gillian was a vision. Her burgundy gown brought out the color that had returned to her cheeks, and her dark hair flowed artfully down her shoulders from her center part. She was reclined comfortably near the fire where she could soak in some much-needed warmth. Still, even with the improvement to the color of her skin and her manner of walking, she tired easily.

At her frown, he asked, "Are you positive you are well enough to join me today?" Concerned about her still-fragile state, Simon had arranged for servants to always be on hand to see to her every need. None were present at the moment, though, because he was in the room. "Would you like me to summon Daisy?"

She shook her head and reached for a cup of tea on a neglected tray before her. By now, the tea was probably cold. "That won't be necessary," she said, then took a sip. "Please do go on. I am quite ready to acquaint myself with all that has transpired."

He cleared his throat, a subtle way of showing her he wasn't as certain as she was. "The sad truth is, we have no way of knowing how far the rabbit has tunneled."

"Simon." Her brows knit together as she placed the empty cup back on the tray.

"Yes, my love?" he asked curiously. "Have you changed your mind about Daisy?"

"No," she said. "I am determined to resume my life, thank you." She raised her chin, exuding calm and focus. "At present, I feel it's my duty to congratulate you on the way you've handled the vicar's interrogation. I doubt there are many men alive who would have been so generous after—"

"Let us never speak of it again, shall we?" A muscle in his jaw twitched as he tried harnessing his irritation. "It is not for want of sending him straight to the devil that he still lives."

"Of course," she said, her tone soothing and light. "I daresay the vicar's secrets are as important to him as vestments and incense." He valued them little.

"Ha!" She had a way of making comparisons that never ceased to amaze him. "In the end, it doesn't matter."

"It never does," she said matter-of-factly. "Did Holt finally break?" She angled her shoulders toward him, her gaze expectant. "Oh, how I wish I could have been there to hear him explain his actions." She lowered her eyes. "What did you learn?"

God, her inquisitive mind intrigued him, heightening his appreciation of her. "He revealed something quite enlightening."

"What?" she asked, lifting her gaze.

"That our beloved vicar is connected to none other than Lord Fleming."

She gasped. "How so? Fleming works for Guildford in the House of Lords. Why, Lady Fleming and Lady Guildford are my good friends! That is to say, as much as a spy can rely on friends . . ." She blinked. "I know them to be good and moral women. Surely, you are not implying they have taken any part in—"

"A man in Fleming's position would not make his wife privy to this. The chance of discovery would be too great, especially with how close Lady Fleming seems to be to Lady Guildford."

"Simon!" she exclaimed. "I confess I am bewildered. Fleming is a man of integrity. No one will believe this charge against him!"

He nodded. "Which is why we must obtain evidence to prove our suspicions."

"But can such evidence be found?" she asked with a furrowed brow.

"Well, we already know that Guildford oversees the Church of England's finances." Simon clasped his hands behind his back. "Melville's keen intelligence, combined with his history of subsidizing the clergy to combat domestic radicals, led him and Douglas to verify a trail of funds moving from St. Dionis Backchurch to a banker on Threadneedle Street. The Home Office alone spends one hundred thousand pounds each year on espionage, parts of which could be extracted to help fund Napoleon's war effort without so much as a brow being lifted. Given Holt's betrayal, it's even more uncertain whether or not more double agents are working right under Guildford's nose."

"But arresting a lord isn't done, Simon," she said before pressing her lips together in a tight line. "Has Holt provided you any proof?"

"Not enough. Bank notes have been planted and processed through Thelluson Frères bank and Schmidt, Meyer et Jollivet. Louis Bayard uses both banks in Paris." Bayard's bourgeois origins, his connection to Wickham, and his thirty-eight aliases made him one of Britain's best spies and the perfect agent to verify Holt's claims.

Gillian pulled her wrap tighter about her shoulders, wincing with the effort. "We cannot give our hand away. It would be suicide."

"I agree." He smiled, enjoying her quick mind. "We must contact Bayard."

"And then?" she asked, an eager exuberance transforming her face.

He moved closer to her. "I've sent agents to the coffee-houses, cafes, and clubs under our surveillance."

She reached for his hand. "Which ones?"

"Chapman has gone to Paternoster Row to question booksellers at Chapter, the coffeehouse there," he said, stroking her hand. "Forsyth has gone to a subscription room on Threadneedle Street in the hopes of obtaining new information regarding Napoleon's affairs. Milford is scouting the merchants at Garraway's. And last but not least, Hamlet is targeting the artistic set at Old Slaughter's."

She tapped her fingers on her book. "So we wait."

"In a manner of speaking." He placed his hand over hers, then raised it to his lips and kissed it. "The only way to take down Fleming is to collect indisputable evidence against him." Even then, a conviction would only amount to a sojourn in prison. "I fear our hands are tied until Seaton returns from Spain and everything we learn is verified."

She sank back onto the cushions, an edge of cynicism lancing her voice. "This will take months."

"I am afraid so," he said, his heart in his hand.

Nothing on a political scale could be accomplished at present. Nelson's demise had put the city and the British government in turmoil. Extraordinary measures had been taken to transport the vice-admiral's body back to London. Royal Mail coaches outfitted in laurel leaves had been dispatched from Lombard Street Gate to transmit the news of victory at Trafalgar and of Nelson's death.

A large public funeral was being strategically planned, as well. First, citizens would begin flocking to Town to celebrate the man who'd been Vice-Admiral Lord Horatio Nelson, valiant hero, not to mention he was Simon's confidant. The vice-admiral's body would lie in state at the Painted Hall in Greenwich. When it finally arrives up the Thames, processions will flood the streets on the way to Whitehall. The whole affair will be a demonstration of power, sorrow, and thanksgiving unmatched.

"I cannot rest while the culprit who wants you dead is still at large, Simon," Gillian admitted. "But you are here now, and that, at least, brings me great joy."

"And if I have anything to say about it, we will never be parted from this minute onward."

"That is my prevailing hope, as well, but I am a practical woman." She turned her head briefly and brushed the back of her hand across her lips. "The admiral's body has yet to arrive, and his funeral may not take place until after the new year. If Fleming is responsible for blackmailing Holt and targeting our members, it feels wrong, somehow, to plan a wedding."

"Marrying you is not wrong," he said. She looked back at

him, and together they smiled in earnest. He admired her beauty and strength, cherished her loyalty, and would never allow himself to forget that he'd almost lost her. "But I am a patient man, Gillian."

"Yes," she said swiftly. "Yes, I know."

"Would you prefer to wait until after the admiral's funeral?" he asked. He would do anything to please her. "You have only to say the word."

"No. I want nothing more than to be your wife at last, Simon." The heartrending tenderness in her gaze undid him. He bent down and brushed his lips against hers. "After all, Madame Bernard will be arriving within the hour to measure me for my wedding gown. I cannot just send her away."

He kissed her forehead, the tip of her nose, her eyelids, and finally, her supple lips. "I would marry you without any clothes."

"Simon!" She pushed against his chest, teasing him as laughter found her eyes. "In front of witnesses?"

"No." He grinned. "Save your treasures for me." The heat of her body and the thudding of his own heart were driving him wild. He pulled her toward him and held her, careful not to put any pressure on her wound as he placed a kiss on her hair. "I am the luckiest of men," he reminded her. She gazed up at him, and he gently kissed her lips again, enjoying their velvety texture. "How I long to make a life with you."

"It is what I desire most, Simon. And nothing, including politics and pretense, will ruin our wedding day."

"I will ensure it," he vowed.

"How?"

He stood, then gently helped her to her feet, careful to monitor her expression for any signs of pain. "Not only will our wedding day be of immense joy to both of us but the event will coax the enemy into a false sense of security." He winked and stroked a ringlet of hair that draped over her shoulder.

"Good intelligence is not won by aggression, but by patience and the concealment of one's true intentions." She quirked her brow at him. "What do you plan to do, my lord?"

He winked again and lifted her until he was holding her in his arms. "To conspire to love you for all of my days, that is my strategy." He felt her uneven breathing on his cheek as he held her close.

A tap came at the parlor door, and Goodayle cleared his throat. "Your pardon, my lord. Madame Bernard has arrived for the baroness's fitting."

She gazed up at him. "It appears your strategy will have to wait," she said, twirling his queue.

He burst out laughing. "Well played, my lady. Well played."

"Though I cannot take credit for Madame's arrival, I will never tire of your laughter."

Their eyes met and gazes locked. As she smiled up at him, his buoyant spirits soared and a peace unlike any he'd ever known descended upon him. They would be all right, the two of them. Their lives had taken twisted turns, but no matter what befell them, he and Gillian had returned to each other in extraordinary fashion. Was it Fate or divine intervention?

His heart thundered. "I cannot wait until the day that I can call you mine."

"I *am* yours, Simon," she said as she studied him seductively. "I have always been yours."

His heart swelled. "Then let's not keep Madame Bernard waiting."

Epilogue

But let not Britain, though thus doom'd to bear
Such ponderous misfortunes, yet despair.
Warriors and statesmen still for her shall rise,
Like those whose noble souls have sought the skies;
With generous strife each loyal breast shall glow
To recompense her losses—soothe her woe.
Around the Constitution all shall cling,
Warm in attachment to their virtuous king;
Firm in their resolution to oppose,
With heart and hands united, Britain's foes.
~ "The Triple Loss," Thomas Scott, *The Gentleman's Magazine*, Vol. LXXVI, February 1806

Number Eleven Bolton Street
Three weeks later

As predicted, the Admiralty was forced to postpone Nelson's funeral until after the new year because his body had not yet sailed up the Thames. Lord Seaton's activities were unknown, as he still had yet to return from San Sebastian. At least his absence, and the critical intelligence he'd been ordered to acquire from Don Vasquez, delayed further action on the part of Lord Fleming.

In the interim, guards had been placed at Habersham Place—Lord Guildford's residence—Fleming's townhouse, the House of Lords, and various clubs and taverns Fleming frequented. Detailed intelligence was passed through numerous networks until it reached Simon and Gillian, while Melville and Douglas continued to scour accounts in Whitehall, St. Dionis Backchurch, and Threadneedle Street, hoping to gather the proof they needed.

Meanwhile, Gillian's health had steadily improved. Madame Bernard had been summoned back to the townhouse. The modiste had arrived with a caravan of seamstresses to fit Gillian for new gowns. Simon's niece, the Duchess of Blendingham, and Lady Adele Guffald frequently called for tea. Their presence had been a welcome treat to Gillian and had offered her an opportunity to hear the latest gossip.

Simon paced the Turkish carpet in the Bolton Street townhouse study, taking time to stop and peer at the mantel clock before resuming the practice that helped to calm his nerves. Thankfully, he wasn't alone. Their wedding day had finally arrived, and he couldn't be happier to share it with those members of Nelson's Tea who had become more like family to Simon and Gillian—the Duke and Duchess of Blendingham; Captain and Lady Guffald; Simon's brother, Byron, the Duke of Throckmorton; and Goodayle. Rock had procured a special license for them from Charles Manners-Sutton, the Archbishop of Canterbury in Doctors' Commons, and the private ceremony would be officiated by Mr. Crofton, the very same vicar who'd handled the funerals of Chauncey and Edwina at St. Luke's in Chelsea.

But now he felt the very opposite of what he'd felt about those miserable times and unfortunate events. Simon couldn't have been happier. After loving and losing Gillian all those years ago, they were finally going to be given a second chance at love. Almost two fortnights had passed since he'd nearly lost her. Gillian's wounded side had begun to heal, giving her occasional twinges of pain as she walked the grounds. Together, they'd continue Nelson's work, which was far from over.

"The Third Coalition has come to an end," he said. He was as nervous as he'd been his first day at Eton, though he couldn't explain why.

Blendingham grumbled. "Napoleon's Grand Armée has won a decisive battle in Ulm."

"Don't waste another moment worrying about treaties and campaigns and hostile emperors," Guffald said. "Today is a joyous day. War and its burdens can wait."

Yes. He had wasted too much time as it was.

The ormolu clock chimed ten times.

Goodayle appeared in the doorway. "It's time, my lord."

Simon adjusted his cuffs and glanced at Blendingham, who was dressed in embroidered gold and cream. The duke cocked his hip at an odd angle in front of Simon's brother, Rock, and then flipped open his quizzing glass. "Well, what are you waiting for, my good man?"

"It is a great day for a wedding, if I do say so myself." Rock cleared his throat. "You've both been given a second chance to change your destiny; you have no idea how I envy you that. Take it from someone who knows, Brother. Marry the woman you love. Life ends too soon."

Simon's throat bobbed as he swallowed thickly, tightening his cravat around his neck. He stepped toward his brother and put his hand on his shoulder. "Thank you, Rock."

Constance, who stood next to her father and husband, smiled broadly. "You and the baroness deserve every happiness, Uncle."

Anticipation filled him as he waited beside the vicar, longing to get his first glimpse of his wife-to-be.

A dainty silver slipper appeared in the doorway, emerging

out from under yards of gathered white silk accentuated with an overlay of intricately spun lace in the palest lilac. A silver ribbon adorned Gillian's waist, leading his gaze to her trimmed bodice where interlocking silver ribbons crossed her breast. A starched, pale-lilac collar rose from the gown's neckline, fanning her face and accentuating her dark-chocolate eyes. Ringlets cascaded along her brow, poking out from beneath a silver silk turban lined with lavender flowers.

She was a vision cloaked in mist. Her radiant, beaming smile as she accepted his outstretched hand bespoke nothing of the hardship she'd endured these many weeks. She was the strongest woman he knew, a force to be reckoned with. She'd shown her mettle by more than half, gained a title, and helped save Nelson's life, years earlier.

Simon broke into a smile as love coursed through him. His heart pounded an erratic rhythm. Indeed, he was the

GILLIAN WAS FILLED with excitement as she studied the man who'd captured her heart offstage at Drury Lane so many years ago. His double-breasted slate jacket, silver waistcoat, white cravat, and trousers fit him to perfection. Candlelight glimmered over his handsome face, and the humor touching his mouth crinkled the corners of his eyes, making her belly tighten and her senses take flight. She'd been a fool not to wait for Simon. But if she hadn't married Lucien, she might never have found him again. Now, before a man of God and a crowd of witnesses, she was finally pledging her troth to her soul mate. It was—they were—a dream come true.

"I apologize for keeping you waiting, my lord," she said, admiring the set of his shoulders before nodding to their friends and loved ones.

"Never," he said, caressing her fingers. "You are here now, with me, and that is all that matters."

How she wished her mother were here to share this moment with them. Other than her mother's, Lucien's, and Simon's love, she had experienced few relationships as powerful as the tug the members of Nelson's Tea had given her heart. In this present company, she felt buoyant and free, yet as her eyes clung to Simon's, her pulse pounded.

Mr. Crofton coughed perceptibly to gain their attention, then began reciting *Fordyce's Sermons*. Gillian barely heard the vicar. She'd heard marriage readings at other weddings, in another life. Instead, the world beyond Simon's eyes dimmed as she concentrated on the man she loved, the one she'd nearly died for.

Powerful relief filled her as he held her hands before them, his gaze brimming with tenderness and passion as he leaned toward her. Her heart was filled with gratitude. She drank in every nuance of him: his bold and loving gaze, his aquiline nose, his strong jaw, and the breathless, deepening love that linked them with such an intimate thread. He was all that was good and just, noble and compelling, and worthy of more than she could possibly give him, especially children.

A shadow of grief washed over her. Only one thing terrified her in this world anymore—her inability to have children. Oh, how she prayed Russell was wrong!

She briefly closed her eyes, then reopened them, despising the tear that slipped down her cheek. This was the happiest of moments. A knot formed in the pit of her stomach, banding her insides like the ring that Simon would soon place on her finger.

"Is something wrong?" he whispered, tightening his grip on her hands.

Crofton immediately stopped reading and looked at her, too surprised to do more than nod. "Are you unwell, my lady?"

"I am quite well, Mr. Crofton," she said, gazing down at the hands that held hers. "I am a little light-headed, that is all. You see, I have dreamed of this day for such a long time that I cannot believe any of this is real."

"As you can see," Simon said, lifting her chin, "I am very real."

She shuddered as warmth flowed over her like honey. Was it wrong to be genuinely happy, in spite of what was happening in the world? Her pulse quickened at the speculation.

Simon placed her hand atop his elbow and turned toward Mr. Crofton.

"Are you ready to proceed, Baroness?" The vicar spoke softly so only they could hear as he pushed his spectacles up the bridge of his nose.

"I am." Gillian glanced up at Simon. "Very much so."

"Brilliant." Mr. Crofton beamed. "Dearly beloved, we are gathered here to join together this man and this woman . . ."

As Mr. Crofton recited the matrimony service, Gillian gave in to the glorious wonder that had filled her all day, basking in Simon's love, cherishing his devilishly handsome looks. His dazzling smile claimed her completely, pushing back the fears she carried with her.

She smiled back at Simon in earnest as Mr. Crofton said, "Who giveth this woman to be married to this man?"

Blendingham, Gillian and Simon's fondest friend, stepped forward and tipped his quizzing glass as he bowed. "I do."

Gillian's heart soared as Simon repeated his vows. So lost in the moment was she that she wasn't aware it was her turn to speak until Simon placed her right hand over his.

Her troubled spirits quieted. "I, Gillian Stillman Corbet, take thee, Simon Danbury, to be my wedded husband." Her heart took a perilous leap. "To have and to hold from this day forward, for better or for worse, for richer or poorer, in sickness . . . and in health, to love, cherish, and to obey, 'til death do us part, according to God's holy ordinance, and thereto I give thee my troth."

Simon placed a family ring—an amethyst surrounded by diamonds—midway on her finger. "With this ring," he said, "I thee wed. With my body, I thee worship. And with all my worldly goods, I thee endow. In the name of the Father, and of the Son, and of the Holy Ghost. Amen."

Gillian gazed down at the fourth finger on her left hand in wonder as Mr. Crofton continued speaking. "For so much as Lord Danbury and Baroness Chauncey have consented together in holy wedlock, and have witnessed the same before God and this company, and thereto have given and pledged their troth either to other, and have declared the same by giving and receiving of a ring. And by joining of hands, I pronounce that they be man and wife together, in the name of the Father, and of the Son, and of the Holy Ghost. Amen."

Gillian drank in Simon's leather-and-spice scent as he embraced her with agonizing slowness and care. She desired his lips upon hers but knew this wasn't the place or time for such an intimate gesture.

Simon must have read her mind. He drew back, cupping the sides of her face. "I love you, Wife."

Her skin tingled where he touched her, and her eyelashes fluttered against her cheeks as she closed her eyes, luxuriating in his nearness. "And I love you, Husband."

In one swift motion, he drew her face toward his.

She broke away. "My lord, do you mean to scandalize me in front of family and guests?"

He winked. "That would be an impossible feat."

"With you," she said, gazing into his startling gray eyes, "everything is possible."

Mr. Crofton cheered, "Hear, hear!"

The others joined in.

Gillian beamed, unable to suppress her happiness, as she accepted congratulations bestowed on them by those she loved and adored. This was the day she'd always dreamed of. Euphoria filled her as she stood by Simon's side. They were two hearts, two minds, bonded by Fate, secrets, and danger. But together, come what may, the risks they'd taken had eventually led them home.

Thank you for reading *My Lady Rogue*!

Dear Reader,

Reviews are a great way for readers like you to find books, and I'd be ever so grateful if you shared your experience with others.

I hope you enjoyed the fourth book in my Nelson's Tea Series!

Thank you for reading!
Katherine Bone

Interested in knowing when the next book will be available? Sign up for Katherine's Rogues, Rebels & Rakes E-Newsletter.

www.katherinebone.com/contact

Author's Note

While researching my historical novels, I always find interesting tidbits of history to use in my books, and I confess to being fascinated by Vice-Admiral Lord Viscount Horatio Nelson, his life, and his military career. What better way to convey the emotions of November 6, 1805, than to include poems depicting Nelson's life and death, as well as the deep respect and adoration for England's most beloved hero of the age.

During the Napoleonic Wars, Nelson's victories were legend, whether or not one agreed with his tactics. In *My Lady Rogue*, I took literary license by tweaking the Trafalgar Way route that Lieutenant John Lapenotiere took to deliver dispatches with news about the victory at Trafalgar and Nelson's death. I added my fictional character, Lord Garrick Seaton, to the post chaise on its seventh stop to obtain fresh horses at Exeter. I understand that adding another passenger in the post chaise might slow the four-horse-drawn vehicle, especially since he was competing with Commander John Sykes for the privilege of arriving first. But in keeping with the timetable Lapenotiere had established—a 271-mile journey necessitating twenty-one horse changes—I did not account for the added weight in this book.

The traumatic loss of Admiral Nelson—the "ideal romantic death," according to Andrew Lambert, Professor of Naval History at Department of War Studies, King's College, London—was felt throughout England and across the economic divide. A national state of mourning commenced, rivaling royal deaths as Nelson was laid to rest at St. Paul's Cathedral. Collingwood's dispatches were shared with the public. Poems and songs were written to honor Nelson and his victory at Trafalgar. Statues were erected of him in the coming years, as well—less than half still remain today—and Trafalgar Square opened in 1843. Two hundred streets bear Nelson's name or reference the Battle of Trafalgar in the United Kingdom. And every October 21, the Royal Navy celebrates Trafalgar Night on board *HMS Victory*, the oldest commissioned ship in the world, which is permanently dry docked at Number 2 of the Royal Navy Museum in Portsmouth. Port, Nelson's favorite liquor, is imbibed and toasts are given to the "immortal memory of Admiral Nelson."

We can only imagine a world where information passed slowly. Imagine receiving a dispatch announcing the information you'd been longing to hear, only to experience the deepest sorrow amid news of victory. Collingwood's dispatch, which I've included in full following this letter, grips my muse. It's a powerful testament to the bravery of one man leading a fleet and a nation—the man who inspired Nelson's Tea.

Resources used in my research included the following:

Colchester Men Who Fought at the Battle of Trafalgar:
     www.camulos.com/trafalgar.htm

Royal Museum Greenwich: www.nmm.ac.uk

Wikipedia: en.wikipedia.org/wiki/The_Trafalgar_Way

Old Maps of Exeter, England:
     www.oldmapsonline.org/en/Exeter

The National Archives: www.nationalarchives.gov.uk

The Great Trafalgar Dispatch Mystery: www.sam-willis.com

The Battle of Trafalgar, (10/21/1805): Vice Admiral Cuthbert
     Collingwood's Dispatch: www.admiralnelson.org

Royal Tars by Brian Lavery

The Naval Chronicle, Vols I–III, edited by Nicholas Tracy

Jack Tar by Roy and Lesley Adkins

Poems From www.rc.umd.edu/warpoetry/1805

> "Horatio's Death," Anon, *The Morning Chronicle* (11/22/1805)

> "Nauticus," The Battle of Trafalgar, (10/21/1805) *The Gentleman's Magazine*, Vol. LXXV (11/1805), pp. 1044–1045

"The Muffled Drum," John Mayne

> *The European Magazine*, Vol. XLVII (7/1805), p. 51

> *The Gentleman's Magazine*, Vol. LXXV (7/1805), p. 656

> *The Monthly Mirror*, Vol. XX (8/1805), p. 126

> *The Morning Chronicle*, (8/17/1805)

"Epicedium on the Death of Lord Nelson," S. Buller

> *The Gentleman's Magazine*, LXXV (11/1805), p. 1046

> *The Poetical Register and Repository of Fugitive Verse, V* (1807), p. 283

Vice-Admiral Cuthbert Collingwood's Dispatch

To William Marsden Esq., Admiralty, London
Euryalus, off Cape Trafalgar, Oct. 22.

Sir,

The ever to be lamented death of Vice Admiral Lord Viscount Nelson, who, in the late conflict with the enemy, fell in the hour of victory, leaves to me the duty of informing my Lord Commissioners of the Admiralty, that on the 19th inst. it was communicated to the Commander in Chief from the ships watching the motions of the enemy in Cadiz, that the combined fleet had put to sea; as they sailed with light winds westerly, his Lordship concluded their destination was the Mediterranean, and immediately made all sail for the Streights' entrance, with the British squadron, consisting of twenty-seven ships, three of them sixty-fours, where his Lordship was informed by Captain Blackwood (whose vigilance in watching, and giving notice of the enemy's movements, has been highly meritorious) that they had not yet passed the Streights.

On Monday, the 21st instant, at day light, when Cape Trafalgar bore E. by S. about seven leagues, the enemy was discovered six or seven miles to the eastward, the wind about west, and very light, the Commander in Chief immediately made the signal for the fleet to bear up in two columns, as they are formed in order of sailing; a mode of attack his Lordship had previously directed, to avoid the inconvenience and delay in forming a line of battle in the usual manner. The enemy's line consisted of thirty-three ships (of which 18 were French and 15 Spanish) commanded in chief by Admiral Villeneuve; the Spaniards under the direction of Gravina, wore, with their heads to the northward, and formed the line of battle with great closeness and correctness;-but as the mode of attack was unusual, so the structure of their line was new; it formed a crescent convexing to leeward-so that, in leading down to their centre, I had both their van and rear, abaft the beam; before the fire opened, every alternate ship was about a cable's length to windward of her second a-head, and a-stern, forming a kind of double line, and appeared, when on their beam, to leave a very littler interval between them; and this without crowding their ships. Admiral Villeneuve was in the Bucentaure in the centre, and the Prince of Asturias bore Gravina's flag in the rear; but the French and Spanish ships were mixed without any apparent regard to order of national squadron.

As the mode of our attack had been previously determined on, and communicated to the Flag Officers and Captains, few signals were necessary, and none were made, except to direct close order as the lines bore down. The Commander in Chief in the Victory led the weather column, and the Royal Sovereign, which bore my flag, the lee.

The action began at twelve o'clock, by the leading ships of the columns breaking through the enemy's line, the Commander in Chief about the tenth ship from the van, the Second in Command about the twelfth from the rear, leaving the van of the enemy unoccupied; the succeeding ships breaking through, in all parts, astern of their leaders, and engaging the enemy at the muzzles of their guns: the conflict was severe; the enemy's ships were fought with a gallantry highly honourable to their officers, but the attack on them was irresistible, and it pleased the Almighty Disposer of all Events, to grant his Majesty's arms a complete and glorious victory.

About three P.M. many of the enemy's ships having struck their colours, their line gave way: Admiral Gravina, with ten ships, joining their frigates to leeward, stood towards Cadiz. The five headmost ships in their van tacked, and standing to the southward, to windward, of the British line, were engaged, and the sternmost of them taken:-the others went off, leaving to his Majesty's squadron, nineteen ships of the line, (of which two are first-rates, the Santissima Trinidad and the Santa Anna) with three Flag

Officers, viz. Admiral Villeneuve, the Commander in Chief, Don Ignatio Maria D'Aliva, Vice Admiral, and the Spanish Rear Admiral Don Baltazar Hidalgo Cisneros.

After such a victory it may appear unnecessary to enter into encomiums on the particular parts taken by the several Commanders; the conclusion says more on the subject than I have language to express; the spirit which animated all was the same; when all exerted themselves zealously in their country's service, all deserve that their high merits should stand recorded; and never was high merit more conspicuous than in the battle I have described.

The Achille (a French 74), after having surrendered, by some mismanagement of the Frenchmen took fire and blew up; two hundred of her men were saved by the tenders.

A circumstance occurred during the action, which so strongly marks the invincible spirit of British seamen, when engaging the enemies of their country, that I cannot resist the pleasure I have in making it known to their Lordships; the Temeraire was boarded by accident, or design, by a French ship on one side, and a Spaniard on the other; the contest was vigorous, but, in the end, the combined ensigns were torn from the poop, and the British hoisted in their places.

Such a battle could not be fought without sustaining a great loss of men. I have not only to lament in common with the British Navy, and the British Nation, in the fall of the Commander in Chief, the loss of a Hero, whose name will be immortal, and his memory ever dear to his country; but my heart is rent with the most poignant grief for the death of a friend, to whom, by many years intimacy, and a perfect knowledge of the virtues of his mind, which inspired ideas superior to the common race of men, I was bound by the strongest ties of affection; a grief to which even the glorious occasion in which he fell, does not bring the consolation which perhaps it ought; his Lordship received a musket ball in his left breast, about the middle of the action, and sent an officer to me immediately with his last farewell; and soon after expired.

I have also to lament the loss of those excellent officers, Captains

Duff, of the Mars, *and Cooke, of the* Bellerophon; *I have yet heard of no others.*

I fear the numbers that have fallen will be found very great, when the returns come to me; but it having blown a gale of wind ever since the action, I have not yet had it in my power to collect any reports from the ships.

The Royal Sovereign *having lost her masts, except the tottering foremast, I called the* Euryalus *to me, which the action continued, which ship lying within hail, made my signals, a service Captain Blackwood performed with great attention; after the action, I shifted my flag to her, that I might more easily communicate my orders to, and collect the ships, and towed the* Royal Sovereign *out to seaward. The whole fleet were now in a very perilous situation, many dismasted, all shattered, in thirteen fathom water, off the Shoals of Trafalgar, and when I made the signal to prepare to anchor, few of the ships had an anchor to let go, their cables being shot; but the same good Providence which aided us through such a day, preserved us in the night, by the wind shifting a few points, and drifting the ships off the land.*

Having thus detailed the proceedings of the fleet on this occasion, I beg to congratulate their Lordships on a victory, which, I hope will add a ray to the glory of his Majesty's Crown, and be attended with public benefit to our country.

I am, &c.
C. Collingwood